THE

UNHEARD

HOUSEWIFE

A Journey from Ashes to Wings

SHEENAM KHAN

SHEENAM KHAN

The Unheard Housewife
A Journey from Ashes to Wings

This is a work of fiction. Names, characters, places, and incidents either are the product of the author's imagination or are used fictitiously. Any resemblance to actual persons, living or dead, events, or locales is entirely coincidental.

About the Author

Sheenam Khan is a young talented Kuwait-based Indian author, known for her significant contributions to K-12 and commercial literature. With a genuine passion for storytelling and an enduring love for the written word, she has enchanted young readers and educators through a varied portfolio that includes best-selling academic books, commercial books, stories, and poems.

She holds a certificate in teaching English as a secondary/foreign language: TBLT approach, from the University of London, UK., along with a masters degree in business administration from St. John' s College, Agra, India. Her deep love for literature shines through in every creation, as she artfully combines creativity, emotion, and imagination.

Through her writing, Sheenam Khan has built a reputation for nurturing a love for reading, promoting critical thinking, and empowering people globally to explore the joys of storytelling.

Other Books by the Author

Sheenam Khan's latest award-winning children's book **'Olivia And Jack Learn About The Touch'**, teaches children an important lesson about personal safety: distinguishing between 'good touch' and 'bad touch'.

The book is crucial for helping children understand boundaries and personal space, empowering them to protect themselves and communicate their feelings effectively.

By understanding the concepts in the book, children can navigate social interactions with confidence and security.

The book has won **Sahitya Sparsh Award for Best Children's book (Fiction).** Hence, proving it to be a must read for parents, teachers and children.

Ram Prasad

"Nandini... Nandini...", called Ram Prasad as he was standing at the main gate of his house with a shovel in one of his hands and a big sack of manure on his head.

"Tell your mother that I'll be late today. There is a lot of work in the fields", said Ram Prasad.

"I knew it. Here, take your lunch box with you and do eat it on time, *baba*", replied Nandini.

Ram Prasad was an old weak man in his 60's. He lived in the village with his family of three. He was a destitute farmer who worked tirelessly to provide for his family. Although Ram Prasad was not educated, he was a man of morals and conscience.

He had not enough funds to hire any person to help him in the fields and nor did he have any equipments for the same. Thus, Ram Prasad did all of the work in the fields by himself which led to his poor state of health and a list of ailments.

He knew about the fact that he won't be able to do all of this for long, so he and his wife *Shashikala* sensibly decided to have only one child as they could barely afford even one.

Despite being unable to cope up with his family expenses completely, he never gave up on his responsibilities of being the man of the house, a husband and a father.

*****

Nandini

Nandini was Ram Prasad and Shashikala's only child. When she was born, Ram Prasad and his wife were so happy. She was considered the blessing of her house.

Looking at the new born's round little face, Ram Prasad decided that he would do everything possible to provide a good life for her precious daughter. They instantly decided to name her *'Nandini' – a woman who brings joy.*

Nandini was a respectful and caring daughter who got mature and practical at a tender age due to her prevailing circumstances. Not only she was good to her parents but in general, she was extremely good to everyone around her.

She was a calm, composed and a very understanding human being.

With a heart full of empathy for all, she used to keep others' happiness before her. That's because Nandini learned by an example.

She was raised by a mother who *always...* always kept others before her.

*****

Shashikala

Shashikala was a lady with homely values. She had always listened to the orders of her husband, served him at all costs, and above all, pushed down all her desires and dreams for the sake of running her family happily.

She adjusted quietly in every situation that came along with her marriage with Ram Prasad without even complaining once. No issue could have wiped off the bright smile from her face.

Looking at her, one could tell that in spite of living a poor life, Shashikala was the happiest wife and a mother who was fully satisfied with what life has given her. She always treated her husband like a pious idol; kept him and Nandini before her – *always*.

*****

Nandini's Education

Ram Prasad sent Nandini to a local girls' high school in the village. He would work extra to pay her fees on time. Nandini was blessed with parents like hers. She used to witness all the sacrifices of them since childhood and this is what made Nandini keep them before her own self.

Nandini was good at studies but this did not work out for her as her school was only till grade 10. After that, those who wanted to study further, needed to go to the city for higher education. Nandini wanted to study further. She wanted to earn for *baba* and *maa*.

She had lots of dreams and hopes to become something in life. Though she was generally a quiet person like her *maa,* she wanted to express a lot.

So, she started writing a diary. She would write in it whenever she would feel sad, scared, emotional or happy. All of her unheard desires and dreams were to be found written in her diary.

Dear diary,

I am nervous and excited at the same time. As you know, today at 10.00 am my grade 10 result will be out. Oh my God! I am thrilled. I don't know what it will be but I believe it will be good as I had studied a lot for it. I can't wait to go to the city for higher education.

Imagine, how will the city be? The people, the things, the vibes... new, fresh and promising! What will I carry with me? I don't have much good clothes and the ones I posses are not even modern but I don't want to ask baba for it. He is already doing too much. Ummm, we will see that later.

*****

Nandini's Result

It was 10.00 am. As they didn't have an internet connection or a smart phone at home, *Baba, maa* and Nandini were at the high school, waiting at the school notice board for the result to be pinned there.

As soon as the results were pinned, a multitude of crowd went closer to get a look. There were lots of parents and students who wanted to check whether they passed or failed 10th. Ram Prasad and Shashikala waited for Nandini to check and tell them the good news.

"Why is she taking a lot of time Shashikala?" asked Ram Prasad.

"There are hundreds of people there. Don't worry, I know she will pass and then, she will get the best *'rishta'* for her", replied Shashikala.

It was a fact that both Ram Prasad and Shashikala were a blessing as parents to Nandini but they too came from a society where educating a girl child was not a norm. It was considered that a girl's only job is to serve the family, raise children and take care of all the household chores. That's what women are created for.

So, for the people in their society, the biggest achievement for a girl was to get married at an early age, bring offspring to this world and look after the husband and house perfectly.

Thus, education in their village was a luxury that only a few girls would get and that too the maximum qualification was only high school. Also, the major reason for teaching girls in the village was to fetch a good alliance for them rather than to make them independent.

Similarly, Ram Prasad and Shashikala wanted Nandini to pass 10th as that would get her a perfect man for marriage. She will be happy for her entire life. That's all they wanted for her – *to be happy!*

Nandini returned to her parents after checking the result and her expressions said it all. Delightfully she said, "I did it baba. Maa I passed grade 10th with good marks. All due to your prayers for me."

Her parents got so happy to hear her achievement. "Thanks to God, now wait and see how my girl will get the best alliances for marriage. The entire village will witness my daughter's destiny. She will lead a life of a princess in her husband's palace," said Shashikala hugging Nandini.

Nandini's face turned from a blushing rose to a shocking pale. She felt like her entire plan for future was burned down. She wanted to achieve so much in life but hearing her mother's plan of getting her married, she was devastated.

That night, Nandini's father brought home her favourite sweet *'jalebi'* as a gift for her achievement.

*****

Nandini's Broken Dreams

As Nandini was laying the mat on the floor for having dinner, she heard *baba* saying to *maa,* "Shashikala, did you call Kaplesh and inform him about Nandini's achievement?" (Kalpesh was the mediator for marriages in their village. He would bring in the suitable alliances for girls and boys accordingly. He had good ties with the families dwelling in the city)

Ram Parsad continued, "If not, call him first thing in the morning tomorrow. A good alliance will take time. We shall start searching now, then only we can find a perfect groom for our Nandini. You know, I am not in the best of my health. I hope I am able to marry her off in front of my eyes. Future is unforeseen and the world is cruel Shashikala. Also, next week I have to go to the city for a deal with a wholesaler. I have to work harder to save money as I don't want to send Nandini to her *sasural* empty-handed."

That night, Nandini was filled with an emotion of helplessness and regret. She wanted to tell *baba* that she wishes to go to the city to study further instead of getting married.

However, she couldn't express her desire for it as she was well aware of the expenditure involved in sending her for further education.

Dear diary,

Today was a big day in my life. I passed grade 10 with good marks. But it is of no use. You know why? Baba and maa wants me to get married. They think that I'll get the best groom as I am a metric pass. Should I laugh at it? Or should I tell them my desire?

Huh! How can I be so selfish? I know baba is doing more than his ability for me.

He worked day and night in his poor health to pay my school fees.

Now how can I ask him to take on my burden for sending me to the city. Maybe, he won't say no but he will struggle with his life just to pay for me. Haven't you seen how happy they are for me? They think their daughter has won the world and will live a happy life with her perfect groom forever.

I can't take that happiness away from them. Not at all!

*****

A Family From City Comes Over for Nandini's *Rishta*

A few months passed and meanwhile, Nandini's mother taught her all the domestic chores of the house like sewing, embroidering, stitching and cooking. Nandini was equally good at all these artistic things. Her interest grew in these activities so much so that she even took up the daily cooking of the house. *Maa* and *baba* were happy to see her running the house perfectly at this young age.

One day, the family was having the breakfast together on the mat. Ram Prasad got a call on his phone. It was Kalpesh.

"Kalpesh *beta*, how are you? That's great. What??? Oh! Today? In the afternoon? Okay... okay... how many people will be coming? No, don't worry, your aunty will prepare everything quickly.

"Okay Kalpesh, see you then." said *baba* on the call.

"What happened? What did he say?" asked Shashikala.

"Shashikala be ready, a family is coming over at our house for lunch today to see our princess, Nandini. Kalpesh didn't give much information on the call but said that they are a well-to-do family, the boy is a bank executive and the only child. Make sure all the preparation is perfect. They should not get a chance to find any shortcoming in our welcome," replied Ram Prasad excitedly.

Nandini's heart almost stopped. It was a mixed feeling. She was confused if she was nervous, happy or sad. She was now an 18-

year-old, ready for marriage but she knew, marriage brings in many challenges with it.

"Wear this saree my child. I have prepared the food. You just have to make a nice tea and when I call you to the living room, come with that and serve the guests okay. And yes, don't forget to use the new tea set that we bought from the fair this year. The golden one. It's kept inside the left cupboard beside the mixer in the kitchen. Okay" said *maa*.

It was 1.25 pm. The guests came over. There were four people. The boy, his mother and his father along with Kalpesh.

"Oh... hello! So nice to see you all. Come this way. I hope there wasn't any problem in searching our house? Sit, sit and be comfortable", greeted Ram Prasad.

"Hello! No there was no problem because

we had a solution named Kalpesh... hahaha... " replied Mukesh, the boy's father who was a retired school teacher and a genuinely, probably the only, nice person in their family. While both the families were having a good time together, Nandini was trying to peep in the living room through the tiny window of her kitchen. She wanted to see the boy.

"Ram Prasad ji, meet our boy Karan. He is working as a bank executive from last 2 years and has now applied for a promotion. Me and his mother Gayatri are lucky to call him our son," said Mukesh.

*****

Karan

Karan was a good-looking man in his late 20s. He completed his masters and had a stable career in a reputed bank. He wanted to marry a girl who suited him in all aspects. A girl with whom he would share his work ideas, go clubbing, movies, trekking, long drives and in parties.

He was not at all ready to marry a less educated village girl who has no idea of city lifestyle and culture. He was only there because of his mother's pressure and for some personal goals.

He had a lot of pretence in his body language and behaviour. One could sense his arrogance and indifference towards people.

*****

Gayatri

"Yes *bhabhiji,* my Karan is so distant from all the ruthless activities that boys of this generation do. Very responsible and respectful boy. Most importantly, he has a heart of gold. Can't even see a mosquito die." acclaimed Gayatri.

Gayatri was a very cunning woman. She had her reasons to visit Nandini for an alliance. Kalpesh informed her that Nandini is a very quiet, mature and naive girl who only does what is said to her. She is great at carrying all the domestic activities since teenage. It feels as if she has no tongue.

Gayatri never wanted her son to get married to a bold and independent city girl. The reason was simple. Karan used to give his entire salary in his mother's hands and a city girl would never tolerate that. She would take

Karan in his possession and his money too, according to her.

On the contrary, a village girl who is only metric pass, silent and has a poor background will never question anything. So basically, the power would always be in Gayatri's hands if she makes Nandini her daughter-in-law.

*****

Nandini Meets Karan

"Where is our lovely little Nandini, aunty? Bring her here," said Kalpesh.

Shashikala went to the kitchen and checked if Nandini took out the tea in the right golden tea set.

"Come fast, greet them and serve them the tea one by one. Walk slow and look down, okay," guided Shashikala to her daughter.

Nandini's heart was racing as she was moving forward to the living room with the tray in her hands. She greeted them all and kept the tray on the table. Then, she started pouring the tea into the cups and served it to them one by one as directed by *maa*.

"Meet my daughter Nandini. She is such a lovely girl. She doesn't speak much and always keep others before her. She knows everything from sewing to cooking. She makes the best sweets in the entire village. In fact, today's sweets are also made by her. Not only domestic things Gayatri ji, she is also 10th pass," said Shashikala proudly.

"Ah! That's great. If she wants to study more, we will help her do that Ram Prasad ji," said Mukesh.

"So pretty and well-mannered. Come here, sit with me Nandini," requested Gayatri.

Karan took a glance at Nandini while she was serving him the tea. He didn't like her at all. She was an average-looking, shy girl who was not at all his type. Moreover, she was only 10th pass. Karan questioned his future with her as a wife. He then looked at his mother who seemed to be content with Nandini.

After having the lunch, it was time for Karan's family to leave. They all bid goodbyes to each other and left. Kalpesh told Ram Prasad that he will inform about the family's decision as soon as they inform him.

Nandini liked Karan. He didn't talk much and seemed to be a gentleman. Perhaps he was a good choice for marriage. After meeting him today, she felt that marriage is not as bad as she thought.

Dear diary,

I don't know what kind of a feeling I had today. Should I lament over my past or prepare for my future. I think I liked that boy Karan. He was good. Seemed like one of those city boys who are modern and intelligent. But you know what made me like him?

His parents said that he has a heart of gold. This is what maa says for me too. I believe the thing that is above all is to be a good human, sympathize with others and feel others' pain. I think Karan would be a good person to spend my life with.

*****

The *Rishta* Gets Fixed

After a few days, Ram Prasad got a call from Mukesh saying that, "Ram Prasad ji, I am glad to tell you that we really liked our daughter Nandini and it's a 'yes' from our side. What about you people? Do you too find our boy suitable for her?"

"Yes, yes...Mukesh ji, Karan is such a nice boy. We think that Karan would be the best choice for our Nandini too. Such a talented and mature boy indeed," replied Ram Prasad.

"So if everything is finalised, lets decide the the day and date for the marriage ceremony. Me and Gayatri were thinking that the sooner the better. Why wait longer to have this happen? We can't wait to bring in our *bahu* home! hahaha," said Mukesh excitingly.

Ram Prasad shared the news with Shashikala, who shed tears thinking of her daughter leaving the house soon.

"Oh no! Shashikala, it's a rule of the universe that a girl has to leave her house and her parents one day and move into her real house. But blessed are those parents who get a son-in-law like Karan. Not everyone gets a good alliance these days you see. Alas! this house will no longer be lively without my little princess but I am happy that she got the boy of her dreams in the name of Karan," Ram Prasad comforted Shashikala.

When *maa* informed this to Nandini, she felt something strange inside her heart. It was a... *new feeling*. She had never felt this before.

Now that marriage was in the plan for her, she was mentally prepared for it and somewhere viewing a future full of love with Karan.

Dear diary,

I am getting married to Karan. There is this strange kind of feeling inside my heart which is indescribable. All of this is just so overwhelming.

On one hand, I am feeling as if somebody is snatching me away from from my parents in the phase of their life when they need me the most. While on the other hand, I am feeling a new desire inflicting inside me, a new hope of building a new relation with a stranger. A stranger... that will be my entire world from now on.

I think I am indeed lucky to get married to a boy like Karan. He has every quality in him. He is an educated, well-mannered, cultured and a quiet man.

Hoping for a beautiful married journey with him ahead!

*****

Gayatri's Demand

The wedding preparations started in both the houses. Invites, menu and decorations were all planned. Ram Prasad was trying to go beyond his limits to make his daughter's wedding ceremony a perfect one.

Meanwhile, Gayatri called Kalpesh and said, "kalpesh, see we are not asking for much. Karan wanted the latest model bullet from a long time. So, ask them to arrange for it. As I said; whatever they will give, will be only used by their own daughter. There is nothing new in this. It's a ritual that is going on from decades in our culture. Also, there is a big difference of education between Karan and Nandini, still we chose her. We could have got any girl from the city with a degree for him. Don't you think?"

"So, somewhere they should also compensate for it.

Their daughter is getting more than she deserves to be honest, Kalpesh. Tell them that we don't want anything for ourselves, just a latest model bullet on which their daughter will roam in the city."

Kalpesh called Ram Prasad and told him about Karan's family's demand of the vehicle. Initially, Ram Prasad and Shashikala disliked the fact that they were demanding something expensive and that too so close to the wedding even when they knew about Ram Prasad's financial status.

However, later they convinced themselves by thinking that it is truly a fact that Karan could have gotten a better option than marrying a girl from a village whose father is a poor farmer but still they chose Nandini.

So, they decided to arrange for it but they were short of time.

Ram Prasad decided to sell a piece of his field to make the payment of the latest bullet which was amounting to 2 lac rupees approximately.

Nandini was witnessing all of this. She wanted to go *baba* and say that she doesn't want to start any relation based on demands and sacrifices but because speaking out for herself or stating an opinion was never in Nandini's traits, she kept quiet.

Dear diary,

I know that dowry is something that is prevalent in our society since ever. This is why people think of a girl child as a burden. They day she is born, marriage is the only thing on her parents' mind.

But how can I blame the culture for it? If I were educated and had a degree, I could have blatantly said 'no' to it. In that case, I would have had a lot of options to go for. I would have been independent. People would have been ready to get their boys married to me at any cost because in return they would have gotten an earning 'bahu'.

If nothing, at least I could have helped baba in sharing the expense of the wedding. Alas! Baba is going through all of this because of me and this thought is killing me from inside.

*****

The Wedding Day

The wedding day was filled with both happiness and melancholy. The ceremony took place in Ram Prasad's field under a huge tent house. The bride and groom were ready for performing the wedding rituals.

Ram Prasad and Shashikala were making sure their son-in-law and his parents were treated like royalty. Gayatri was behaving extremely well with Nandini's parents because she saw her demand standing at the corner of the ground where the entire dowry was displayed - *the dark green bullet.*

Mukesh was so happy to see his son getting married to such an innocent girl.

Karan appeared to be the only one who was *not-so-happy.* It looked like he was forced to wear the wedding garment and come to his own wedding. He didn't look happy or excited.

However, Nandini's happiness, innocence and pure soul reflected from the glow of her face in that red bridal attire. The shyness in her eyes, the blush of anxiety on her cheeks, the goodness of her soul, all made her look beautiful.

It was like a movie full of dreams for her where she was the main character. Indeed, the wedding day is the most precious day in every girl's life. Every girl has a right to feel special on this day as the day belongs entirely to her.

Soon, the priest started chanting the wedding mantras and after completing all the wedding rituals, Karan and Nandini were finally a couple - *a married couple.*

There was a lot of chittar-chatter in the

wedding; like all the other Indian weddings. People having dinner, kids running around all over, girls taking pictures, men talking about news and government and ladies about new fashion trends in the market.

It was then time for Nandini's *bidai.* With heavy hearts, Ram Prasad and Shashikala hugged Nandini and kissed her forehead.

They remembered all the moments spent with their daughter since childhood. All the times like when she was born, when they brought her home from the hospital, when she wanted them to be with her, and many more. Her laughter, her cries and her talks were all etched so deep in her parents' hearts.

Ram Prasad being a father couldn't say much. He was numb from the pain of the daughter's separation but Shashikala couldn't control her emotions. She told Nandini how much she loved and cared for her well-being.

At last, she also advised Nandini that, "My love, my heart, remember that you are not going to your *sasural* alone, you are carrying our respect and dignity too with you. You have to make sure your in-laws are happy with you and your husband comes first for you in everything. Above us, above all. You are leaving this house as our daughter my child, but remember you will only leave that house when you leave this world. You are and will always be our little princess. *Maa* and *baba* will always be there for you. Take care!"

Gayatri made Nandini sit with Karan in the car that was decorated with flowers and off they went to their home, leaving Nandini's childhood behind forever.

*****

The Unexpected Wedding Night

Karan's house was all lit with fairy lights. It was a single-storey house, freshly painted for the occasion. There were many guests who were waiting for the bride and groom's car to arrive at the main door. There was list of after-wedding rituals and events that took place till late night in the family. Finally, after all the things were done, it was the time for bride and groom to head towards their room.

The girls took Nandini to her room first. It smelled like roses as it was heavily decorated with them. The room was an average-sized one with all the necessary furniture that Ram Prasad sent a day before as dowry. Nandini sat on the bed with her face covered with a long veil. The girls left and then, Nandini was all alone in the room.

Her heart was racing. She was nervous,

excited, and all things in between. She was also confused as to what would she talk about with Karan? How should she react when he will speak to her for the first time ever?

Although she was extremely tired from all the wedding chaos, she still wanted to make that night her best night ever emotionally. She believed that it was the time that they both would get to know each other as a person for the first time ever. That was a very special feeling for her. Nandini was also excited to get her wedding gift. She decided that she would always keep it close to her for her entire life, whatever it may be.

While Nandini was lost in dreaming about her upcoming moments with Karan, there was a sudden knock at the door and with that, Karan entered the room. Nandini quickly adjusted her veil nervously.

Karan kept Nandini's bags with all her personal stuff under the table. After changing into his night pyjamas, he came onto the bed and lied down. Nandini was still waiting for him to say something but what he said was not at all what she was expecting that night.

"Nandini, I think its too late. You should go to sleep. It was such a hectic day. Go change and sleep. And yes, rise early tomorrow and go greet mummy the first thing in the morning okay," said Karan in not a loving or polite tone at all.

Nandini felt like all her enthusiasm for the night shattered. She didn't understand why Karan acted that way. She was waiting for him with all her heart and soul.

And what about the 'wedding gift'? Didn't she has a right to be gifted anything by her husband as every other bride? Forget about the gift; what about her basic human desire to know things about her life partner? A sweet simple conversation about the most special day of their lives? Or at least a mere 'compliment' ? But there was – *nothing.*

She quickly realised that it was not going to be the married life she dreamt of. Of course, marriage brings in a lot of challenges to face but in Nandini's case, they started way sooner - *from the very first night itself.*

She managed to take out her saree from the bag without any help in her heavy bridal attire and went to the wash room to change. Then she came and slept beside Karan, who was already terribly asleep. She was trying to sleep so hard but still, something kept her awake.

She was pretty sure by now that Karan was not interested in her. A sea of thoughts was hurling in her mind when she looked at Karan's sleeping face. She remembered what *maa* said... that she should make Karan her entire world, her no.1 priority, above all... above her own parents. But here, Karan didn't even bother to ask if she is okay or if she wants something? If she is happy or if she needs help with something? *If...* not even a single line of comfort, kindness or love.

Thinking about all this, Nandini finally felt asleep.

*****

Nandini's First Day at *Sasural*

Next morning, Nandini woke up early as usual. She had always been a morning person because *baba* used to go to the fields early and Nandini would make him the morning tea. It was a routine which she loved.

After taking a shower, she headed to the living room to greet Gayatri but everyone in the house was asleep.

She sat on the sofa waiting for someone to wake up. She was very hungry. After an hour, Mukesh got up and saw Nandini all decked-up and sitting alone in the living room.

He came to her and put his hand on her head and said, "My daughter got up so early. Why? You must be tired, you should have slept for some more time. See everyone is still asleep in the house."

In response, Nandini shyly replied, "No... papa, I wake up early every day so... its my habit."

Mukesh smiled at her and then he quickly went to Gayatri, woke her up telling that Nandini was awake and was sitting outside alone. "She is a new bride. Go and make her eat the breakfast. She must be hungry. Wake up Karan also, they should have the breakfast together."

Gayatri got up and went to the living room where Nandini was sitting. Seeing Gayatri, Nandini quickly stood up and greeted her good morning as advised by Karan. Gayatri smiled slightly in return and went to Karan's room to wake him up for breakfast. They all had breakfast together. By the evening, a few guests that were still in the house, also left. It was the second night for Karan and Nandini together and still, there was no exchange of sentences between them.

The room was filled with awkward silence and lifelessness similar to the first night. Nandini tried to ask about her another bag just to start a conversation but Karan very easily avoided that by pointing towards the cupboard.

*****

Gayatri and Karan's Coldness Towards the New Bride

The next day, Nandini woke up and went to the kitchen where Gayatri was making breakfast for all. When she saw Nandini standing at the door, she asked her to come in. Nandini greeted her. In response, Gayatri told her that she had made the breakfast for all that day but from then on, this responsibility would be handed over to Nandini. The breakfast, the lunch and the dinner. She must prepare all this on time as they were quite punctual with their meals.

"And yes, I asked the maid to stop coming from next week because she is asking for an unnecessary hike in her pay. So, she will come only this week, okay. I believe you will handle all these household chores very responsibly Nandini, right? This is your home now. That is why we have chosen a daughter-in-law like you. I know you are going to make it heaven," said Gayatri to Nandini.

"Don't worry *mummy ji*. I will handle it all. I won't give you any point to be disappointed at me," replied Nandini ecstatically.

Nandini was so naive that she believed what Gayatri said was really an appreciation of her being skilful at household work. Those few good lines about her, made her day, but little did she know that Gayatri was just transferring the entire load of the house work on Nandini's head very sweetly. She fired the maid because now she had her daughter-in-law in place of it to take care of all these things and that too – *for free!*

Four days passed after marriage and Nandini was missing her *baba* and *maa* badly.

She didn't have any cell phone with her so she went to her room where she saw Karan getting ready to go to work. He took a week's leave for his wedding and it was the day he had to resume working.

"Karan ji, I want to talk to *maa*. Can you please call *baba*? I miss them a lot," said Nandini in a low voice.

"I am getting late for office. Do one thing, call them from the landline that's kept in the living room, okay," replied Karan.

"But I don't know *baba's* number," said Nandini.

"Oh God, who on earth doesn't know one's father's phone number Nandini. Wait, I will write it down for you," replied Karan. He took a piece of newspaper lying on the table and wrote Nandini's father's number on it hastily.

"Here you go, and listen, whenever you wish to call them, just use the landline. Do not wait for me to do that for you, okay. You see I am always busy on my phone regarding work," said Karan.

Nandini took the piece of the newspaper with her and went to call her parents from the landline.

*****

Nandini Lies to *Maa*

Nandini picks up the receiver and dials the number hesitatingly.

The bell rings...

Nandini: Hello... *maa*. I am Nandini. How are you? How is *baba*?

Maa: Hello, *beta*. Everything is good here. You say, how are you? Is everything okay there? How is *damad ji?*

Nandini: Yes *maa*. He is good too. I am also fine here. I am missing you and *baba* a lot... *maa*.

Maa: My dear daughter, we too miss u a lot. Your *baba* has left for work. He was about to call you today. You know what? He was saying that Nandini seems to be so happy with *damad ji* that she forgot us. Hahaha. Oh, I wanted to know what did my princess get as a wedding gift from her husband?... Hello... hello... Nandini?

Nandini: ...Yeah, umm... yes maa. It is a beautiful gold chain. He gave it to me...as soon as he entered the room... *maa*.

Maa: Wow! See you are one lucky girl. Not every girl gets a husband as caring as Karan. Make sure to return him his goodness in the form of serving him and taking his ultimate care, okay.

Nandini: Okay *maa*... Tell *baba* that I will call again to talk to him. I am keeping the phone okay. Bye. Take care.

Maa: Take care my child.

Nandini kept the call with a heavy heart. This time, not because she was missing her parents, but because she felt horribly bad that she had to lie to her *maa* about the wedding gift.

As Nandini was used to keep others'

happiness above hers, she never wanted her parents to get worried due to her married life. Also, the call made her remember that she missed those special moments of her first wedding night.

*****

Nandini's Efforts

In the evening when Karan came home, Nandini thought that it was a great idea to make him tea. This way may be they could start with a little conversation.

She went to the kitchen quickly and made tea for Karan. Then she went to her room with a cup and saucer to serve him the tea.

"Karan ji, I have made this for you. Do you want something to have with it? Shall I make something to eat as well?" asked Nandini excitedly.

Karan took the cup in his hands and as soon as he took a sip from it, he screamed at Nandini saying, "This is tea. I drink coffee. If you didn't know about it then couldn't you ask mummy about it?" Nandini got scared and took the cup away from him nervously.

She said, "Okay, I will make coffee for you within 2 minutes."

"No need now. I am going out with my friends. I'll better take it with them," saying this, Karan went off on his new bullet that Ram Prasad got for him.

Nandini was disappointed with Karan's ruthless behaviour towards her. She felt terrible. He had no softness in his tone and moreover, he was way too ignorant as a husband. She wanted to speak to someone about what was happening with her but there was no one. Of course, she couldn't tell any of it to her parents. Then she remembered her only secret keeper – *her diary,* which she brought in with her personal items from home.

As Karan was not at home now, it was the perfect time for her to write her emotions in her diary. She quickly went to her room and took out the bag with only some items left inside as she had already organized her stuff in the cupboard. She searched for a pen which she got on the bedside table where Karan keeps his little things.

Dear diary,

I am so upset and disappointed. Maa told me to make this man my entire world. Baba outdid his capability in order to satisfy his demands. Everything is going as per his orders then why is he so indifferent towards me? Why is he not gentle, caring and soft like my baba is towards my maa? Why is he never in a good mood with me? Always despising, always... neglecting.

See how this room is so lifeless. Silent. But you know what? I won't give up so easily. I still want to make it happen, make it normal like others, I should give him some time. Maybe... I am judging him very early on. Maybe he has some office tensions... or maybe boys need some more time to get adjusted in an arranged marriage than girls.

What if he is trying his best to be comfortable with a new member in his life but is failing? Umm... I think, I should keep on trying making efforts.

After all, it is my marriage, my life and Karan ji is... my man. That's what maa would have done. May be it will take some time, but one day, it will all be good and merry! I hope...

That night, the family was having dinner together when Mukesh said, "Oh, I forgot to tell you all that today in the noon, Ram Prasad ji called me. He and *bhabhi ji* are missing their little princess a lot. Gayatri, how can you forget that after marriage, the bride has to go to her house for a ritual along with her husband? It has been a week now. I felt very bad on the call that we didn't remember about it. Anyway Karan, visit them tomorrow, okay."

"Papa, you know that I have just resumed my work after a week-long holiday. I can't take any more leaves now. So, it's better if Nandini's father comes here and take her home," replied Karan.

Nandini felt horrible. She was feeling like an unwanted person due to Karan's inconsiderate response .

"What do you mean? It's only a matter of a day *beta*. Plus, it's important that you accompany her as her husband and her parent's *damad*," replied Mukesh.

"Oh ho, my son is speaking correct. You see it is not any local job where you can take plenty of leaves and no one will question you. We should not forget that Karan is the only bread winner for the family currently. And recently we have dealt with a huge expense of a wedding ceremony. From where will my child bring that much money? Can't you see he has lost a lot of weight in all this pressure of running the house. Plus, now there is a new member in his life to take responsibility of financially" said Gayatri to Mukesh.

"Okay, so if that is the case, then me and Gayatri will go with Nandini," said Mukesh to all.

"My knees are not at all in a condition to go anywhere right now. I am still pretty much exhausted from the chores of wedding," replied Gayatri.

Mukesh didn't like what Gayatri said in front of Nandini and after giving Gayatri a tough look he said, "Nandini *beta*, me and you will go to your house tomorrow, okay. Be ready to meet your parents. You must be missing them too I know my child."

Mukesh was the only member in the family with whom Nandini would feel like home. He was similar to her *baba*. She would feel happy and emotionally alive when around him.

The following morning, Nandini got ready in a bright blue saree with a full face of make-up. The reason was to attain some of the attention of Karan who was on his phone. While she was gathering her things to carry home, she was constantly craving for Karan's attention. She wanted him to look at her just once and smile to make her day.

"Nandini my child, come quickly... the car is waiting," called Mukesh while Nandini was lost looking at Karan's face in hopes that he would compliment her look or would ask her when will she be back? But sadly, that didn't happen.

"Go quickly. Papa's calling you. You should have done all this packing last night. Now your are running late. Come on, hurry up!" said Karan in a distasteful tone.

These things which generally might appear as something very little to people like speaking in bad tones, answering sarcastically or not paying attention to the person's basic human emotions and needs, are not 'little'. They are the things which give a foundation to a healthy and a loving relationship, be it any relation but most importantly - *a husband and a wife.*

While Nandini was travelling in the car with Mukesh, she was thinking about the responsibilities that was due on Karan as a husband. He was the one who was supposed to go with her. He needed ask Nandini if she required something. He didn't even give any money to her before leaving.

It was the first time she was visiting her house as his wife. He didn't even care about fulfilling Nandini's basic needs as a husband

*****

The Car Arrives at Ram Prasad's House

The car stopped at Ram Prasad's house. Both he and Shashikala were waiting with open arms to greet their daughter and son-in-law. They couldn't wait any longer. Nandini forgot all her pains and regrets as soon as she saw their happy faces.

"Oh! What a surprise! Welcome Mukesh ji. We were waiting here for so long for you all," said Ram Prasad excitingly. Both the men hugged each other while Nandini grabbed her *maa* like a child who was away from a mother for a long time.

They all went inside. "Nandini, where is *damad ji?* He did not come along with you?" asked Ram Prasad.

"Actually, he took a lot of leaves already from office and now his boss wasn't ready to give him any more. That's why he couldn't come Ram Prasad ji. But he sent you both, lots of greetings and love. Gayatri too," replied Mukesh apologetically.

Shashikala took Nandini to her room to ask about her well-being and her new home. "Tell me my child. You are happy, right? How is *damad ji* with you? And Gayatri ji? Did you adjust yourself there or not? What about..."

Nandini held her *maa's* hand and replied, "*Maa... shhh...* how many questions at once... wait and let me catch a breath... hahaha. Yes, everything is fine, *mummy ji,* papa and karan ji are all so good with me. They treat me like a daughter. Like you and *baba.* Don't be so worried about me all the time. I have grown up *maa.*"

"I am a mother Nandini. You won't understand this feeling unless you become one. Okay. Also, don't you want to show your wedding gift to your *maa*?" said Shashikala.

"*Maa... umm...* I... I forgot to wear it because... I – I was getting late and the car was waiting... ," replied Nandini.

"How irresponsible is that of you Nandini! It is not a normal chain, it is your husband's token of love. How can u forget it like this? It is not about the price of it but the emotions connected to it. You must cherish that gift forever. Keep it close to you all the time. How will *damad ji* feel when he will know that you came without wearing his chain? Not good at all. Nandini, do not repeat such mistakes okay *beta*. These little gestures means a lot for husbands," *maa* scolded Nandini.

But all this while, in the back of her mind, Nandini questioned that if any gesture means a lot for wives too? What about the feelings of wives? Why are people always concerned about men's choices, their desires, their likes and dislikes... just why? Why doesn't anybody talk about women's feelings?

Nandini suddenly realised that *maa* was talking to her, so she quickly said that she won't repeat it again.

The day was over and it was time for them to leave after having the dinner. Ram Prasad quickly ran in and brought a couple of things to keep in the car like a big basket full of fruits, boxes of sweets, and 4 envelopes of money for Nandini, Karan, Muskesh and Gayatri.

"Ram Prasad ji, don't involve yourself into such formalities. Else, I won't come here from next time, I'll only send Nandini. You have just spent a lot for us in the ceremony, this is not done. I won't accept it this time. We are Nandini's parents not in-laws," said Mukesh empathetically.

"This has no value Mukesh ji. It is only a token of respect and nothing else seriously. You are our important guests," replied Ram Prasad.

Before sitting in the car, Nandini went to Ram Prasad and asked him, *"Baba,* for how long do you have to do this all? What's the need? The ceremony is already over. You already sold a piece of land for me. When will you stop doing this all?"

"My child, I will do this until the last day of my life for you. Nobody can stop me from doing this. Not even you. Okay," replied Ram Prasad.

With teary eyes, Nandini hugged *baba* and headed back to her *sasural*.

Gayatri opened the door when they reached back home. She didn't ask about their journey or anything but quickly grabbed the stuff from Mukesh's hands that Ram Prasad had sent. She shamelessly started checking the quality of the fruits and the money in the envelopes.

"Organic. 'Fresh - off - the - fields' fruits. Thousand rupees for each of us and five thousand for Karan. One thing I must say, Ram Prasad ji knows very well how to keep the value of important relationships," she commented happily.

"Nandini, if you want your envelope, you can take it from me any time. As of now, I am keeping all of them safe together with me okay," Gayatri continued.

Nandini nodded her head in a positive. She entered her room and saw Karan sleeping peacefully without knowing if her wife was back or not. He didn't make a single call to ask if their journey was fine or if they'll be back the same day. She changed and went to sleep as she was tired from the journey.

*****

Nandini's Major Realisation About Being Independent

From the next day onwards, Nandini took charge of the entire household responsibilities like cooking, sweeping, mopping, dusting and cleaning. Her entire day would pass out in these chores. She would seldom get time to look after her or to call *maa* and *baba*.

Diwali was approaching. Gayatri had to go to the local market for buying some special grocery items for the upcoming festival. She wanted to ask Karan for some extra money for it but he was taking a shower. Gayatri waited for some time but because she was in a rush, she took the money out from Karan's wallet and decided to tell him after coming back.

After a while, Karan came out of the wash room and got dressed up for work. When he searched for his wallet, he realised that it was short of some money. He wondered who could take it without informing him. Usually, this won't happen as Gayatri would always notify him about anything like this, so he doubted on another member of the house. He called the suspect - *Nandini*.

Nandini was making breakfast for the family. As soon as she heard Karan shouting, she ran to the room frighteningly.

"How dare you take money from my wallet without asking me? You know what is this called? Stealing! I didn't expect this from you. If you needed money for something, you could have asked me for it instead of taking it on your own Nandini," shouted Karan.

"Wh... What are you saying? I... I did not take any money. Why... would I do that?," replied Nandini, tears rolling down her innocent face.

"Oh now come on, don't show me these crocodile tears. If you have done it just accept it. I know you have not seen money before so you couldn't control yourself. You think that... because you are my wife, my wallet is yours. Right?" blamed Karan.

"No... I am not a thief... I am not a thief... my baba didn't raise me a thief. I swear to God I didn't take any money," said Nandini. This was the first time she had a little aggression in her voice because this time, her upbringing was questioned.

Meanwhile Gayatri was back from the market. Hearing the argument, she rushed to Karan's room and asked about the matter. When she knew what happened, she told Karan that it was not Nandini but her. She was the one who took the money out from his wallet.

Karan's face went colourless and he realised that he blamed such a huge thing on Nandini without even asking anything. His undying ego didn't let him apologize to Nandini but he also couldn't face her so he rushed out of the house for office.

Nandini washed her face and got back to cooking. But she was really full of emotions. Anger, frustration, fear, anxiety and sadness altogether engulfed her heart and soul. That day, she very strongly realised what is financial independence and what is its importance in a woman's life.

Dear diary,

I was always taught that people with good hearts always win. But the reality is different. Its people with good money who always win. Today, I realised the importance of money in a woman's life. The need of being financially independent.

Its all my fault. I always blamed it on my circumstances for not making it to the city for studying further. Why did I only think that baba had to bear the expense? There were many other ways to do it.

Instead of asking baba for it, I could have taken an educational loan which I could have repaid after my job. Or I could have applied for a scholarship since I was good at studies.

I could have even joined any government college where the fees is very little but one has to score a good cut-off in the entrance exam. If only I had the will power to make it happen, I am sure I would have done it. Then nobody... nobody in this world would have blamed me for stealing!

I would have earned my own money and spent that on me. I wouldn't have to beg people for fulfilling my basic needs. People's attitude towards me would have been totally different than what it is today. I would have gotten the respect that I deserve.

I thought that the thing I regret the most was missing out the special moments at my wedding night but I was wrong. Now I realise that the thing I regret the most is not being able to be independent. I wish I could go back in time and take the right decision for myself!

*****

Karan Makes up for His Fault

Festivities were around the corner. People were decorating houses, bringing flowers and stuff for diwali. It was Nandini's first diwali at her in-laws house. But Nandini wasn't expecting anything from them due to her failed earlier expectations.

In fact, now she was not even trying to initiate any conversation with Karan because after that 'wallet' incidence, she knew her value in Karan's eyes. She thought that no matter how much she tries to mend this relation, men like Karan would never approve her as a wife. So, she stopped looking out for his attention.

Karan was feeling the after-effects of that incident too. It was quite obvious from Nandini's lack of interest in him. Karan's male chauvinism wasn't happy with this new change. He wanted Nandini to keep satisfying his ego by revolving around him for his approval like before.

It was lunch time and Karan was helping Gayatri in fixing the diwali lights when Mukesh came in.

"Beautiful! Now it feels like diwali. Oh, anyway it is our *bahu's* first diwali. What are we doing for her? Karan have you taken her out for diwali shopping yet?"asked Mukesh.

Karan replied, "Papa, I will do that today. I have taken a leave from office to take Nandini out for shopping... just a few things left for decorations and then we'll leave."

"Perfect!" exclaimed Mukesh.

Nandini was listening to this conversation from the kitchen. She couldn't believe her ears.

For the first time ever, Karan agreed to do something for her alleged wife. But why? Why this 'all of a sudden' change in him? Anyway, even after letting go of her *wifey* emotions, somewhere deep down the line, Nandini was excited... *again...* to go out with her husband.

"Nandini, be ready by 5 O'clock. We have to go for diwali shopping okay,"said Karan to Nandini who was doing dishes after lunch.

Nandini nodded in a 'yes'.

Strangely, even after deciding in her mind that there is no use of appealing her husband any more, Nandini still tried her best to look good while getting ready – *to beg for Karan's attention yet again!*

Poor Nandini, she was a woman after all who did not want to lose any opportunity to turn her relation into normal. After all she was her *maa's* daughter!

The activities which are pretty casual for other wives to carry out daily were like a boon for Nandini. Sitting behind Karan on the bullet, holding his shoulder, him asking her if she sat properly... was all a – *new and exciting* – feeling for her.

*****

Karan's Ugly Tactic

Karan took Nandini to the metropolitan area where there were gigantic malls, big cinemas and cool cafés. Nandini was mesmerised by the city lights.

He stopped at one of the malls. He then entered a brand's outlet to buy ethnic wear for the festival. The staff of the showroom was talking in English. Nandini felt hesitated as the vibe over there was really different from her village market.

Karan was a clever man. He knew that Nandini would not be comfortable at a place like that. He didn't bring Nandini to make her experience all of this or to make her happy but to make her realise the modern 'status' of her husband whom she was ignoring after that incident.

First, after trying 3-4 things on him, he selected a nice outfit for himself by asking the lady staff about which one was looking perfect on him. This cheap stunt was also done by him to show Nandini that he can have modern, city girls' attention on him if not Nandini's. He was doing this all just to bring Nandini back on her previous behaviour where she would be always serving him and lying at his mercy for minor approvals.

After he was done for himself, he asked Nandini to choose anything she likes from the store. Nandini took a look at the collection but couldn't find anything for her. Everything there was majorly either '*backless*' or '*sleeveless*' which she was not comfortable with.

"I can't wear any of these. Can we ask for a saree?" asked Nandini.

"I should have known this. You have never seen clothes like these. In the village, where can one see a collection like this? I understand, don't worry. We' ll go somewhere else to buy something that suits your personality," replied Karan.

Karan's tone was sarcastic. Instead of making his wife feel comfortable and confident, he demeaned her intentionally. What a crap of a husband was he! A BIG RED FLAG!

From there, Karan took Nandini to another shop. On the way, Nandini could see several showrooms of pretty sarees. However, Karan stopped at a tiny local market shop. He put the bullet on stand and got inside the shop with Nandini. The shop didn't seem to have quality collection.

"Hello ma'am, what should we show you?" asked the salesman.

"*Umm...* show some regular, heavy work saree,"

replied Karan.

The salesman showed them a lot of options. But the fabric was low quality and the colours were dull. Prices were also cheap. Nandini was confused. She didn't like any of them but had to choose one.

"Sir, why don't you help ma'am to choose the one that looks best on her,"asked the salesperson.

"Ah... take that pink one. It looks good out of all," said Karan uninterestingly to Nandini.

She finalised the pink one. Although that was the one she liked the least, but still she chose it because Karan liked it the most. After all, Nandini couldn't easily give up on her habit of relying on Karan's approval for everything.

Shopping was done. They were on their way back home when Karan stopped at a fancy restaurant to have dinner. It was night by the time they finished shopping so he was extremely hungry.

They went inside and the waiter gave the menu to Karan. It was a Thai restaurant. It was not that Karan would always come to such fancy restaurants to eat but this time he chose it for a reason. He didn't even bother to pass the menu to Nandini as he felt that she would have never heard a single dish from it.

He ordered a *tom yum soup, grilled prawns, seafood salad* and *jasmine steamed rice* for two, all of which Nandini was truly hearing for the first time. He could have at least asked Nandini if she was comfortable eating a new cuisine. But then, how would he make Nandini feel inferior and yearn for his attention back again after witnessing his grandeur?

The food arrived and it seemed *weird* to Nandini. She was really hungry but... it was not easy for her to eat what was present on the table. At first, she hesitated but then, she tried gulping it down her throat. She didn't want Karan to feel bad. He was doing his best that day to treat innocent Nandini with *good things,* even if not her way.

Somehow, she managed to eat a good portion of the food. When they were done, they headed home.

Dear diary,

I got a little hopeful today. For the first time ever after marriage, I felt like a 'wife'. I felt as if our relation is not completely dead but a bit alive. He took me out for shopping and dinner. The saree I got for myself is ironically the colour I hate the most but I think it suits me. That's what he said. You know I tried that weird food I see on TV shows. Something... praw-... I don't know but it was not as bad as it looked.

I believe things have started to go in the right direction. Even if it was not a prefect outing with him, at least we did something what people do as a married couple. Is it a sign that things will soon be okay between us? To be honest, I am very positive for my future now.

*****

Sasural's First Diwali

Two days later, it was diwali. Nandini's first in her *sasural.* She got up earlier than usual as she had to do a lot. Several guests would be coming over at her house today. She had to prepare the food, sweets and look after all the arrangements. She wore the saree and got ready with a zeal.

For the entire day, she was in her real room – *the kitchen* – happily serving them all. While she was taking out food in serving bowls, she heard Mukesh screaming with joy.

"Oh! Welcome Ram Prasad ji and *bhabhi ji.* Happy diwali. What a pleasant surprise!"

"Happy diwali Mukesh ji and Gayatri *bhabhi.* We couldn't resist meeting you all on this auspicious day."

"Where's *damad ji* and our lovely daughter?"asked Ram Prasad.

Nandini came out rushing of the kitchen and hugged *baba* then *maa*.

"What a surprise *maa!* You didn't even tell me. I am glad to see you both," said Nandini tearfully.

Karan entered the living room and greeted Nandini's parents. As usual, they brought a lot of expensive gifts for Karan and his family, along with envelopes.

"Oh ho! Shashikala *bhabhi*, this is not done every time. Some day, leave it for us to serve you too," said Gayatri.

"It's an occasion of diwali. This is just our way of showing love for you all... Specially for our *damad ji*. Hahaha," replied Shashikala.

They all had dinner together and then sat down for conversations. Nandini felt a very strong change in *baba's* personality. He seemed extremely weak and pale. His facial bones were poking out as if there was minimal flesh left.

Concerned, Nandini asked, *"Baba*, what happened to you? All your weight is gone. You look extremely weak and dull. Is everything okay?"

"Yes, my child. You have seen me after a long time that's why you feel the change. I am all good. If you doubt, ask your *maa*. Don't worry about me. You better take care of yourself. By the way, you look so beautiful today, my princess," replying this, Ram Prasad kissed Nandini's head.

Although Ram Prasad tried his best to ensure Nandini of his fit health but Nandini, being a daughter, could sense that something was wrong with *baba*.

Cheers and laughters filled the living room. But then it was time for Nandini's parents to leave.

Little did Nandini know that it was the last time she was seeing *baba*.

*****

Karan's Erratic Behaviour & Gayatri's Wish of a Grandchild

Things went back to routine after the week of diwali. Offices and schools were reopened. But something that caught Nandini's attention was Karan's erratic behaviour.

Instead of things turning towards the right direction as expected by Nandini, they turned even more wrong. But this time, even Gayatri was noticing the change.

Karan started behaving strangely with everyone, not just Nandini. He started coming late at nights and leaving much earlier for office. He was frustrated all the time. He even stopped giving his complete salary to Gayatri but only a portion of it to run the house. Upon asking, he said that it's only a matter of some days and then he will be able to give double the salary at home. Apparently, he was working on something for his promotion at bank.

One fine afternoon, Gayatri came back from the hospital where she went to see her neighbour's new born grand daughter and she appeared to be upset.

"What happened *mummy ji*? You look tensed," asked Nandini concerned.

"Why will I not be concerned. It has almost been a year now to your marriage and we have still not got to hear the 'good news' from you. When will we get the opportunity to see our grandchild's face. Don't know how much time is left for us in this old age. I have only one son. I don't understand why today's girls don't want to expand their family on time. Bharti's son got married ten months back and see, today their daughter is born. Lucky are those mothers," replied Gayatri in a disappointed tone.

Nandini had no answer to that. She wanted to scream and tell Gayatri that why doesn't she ask the same question to her son? Is that decision something to be taken alone by Nandini? Who will tell this mother that her son is not even interested to *talk* to his wife, he has not even given the position to her of being a *wife* in his life yet, let alone taking such a big step further of expanding his family with her.

Nandini left after saying, "Things happen on their right time *mummy ji*. Do not worry. Take care of yourself."

*****

Baba's Death

A week later, it was around 10.45 pm in the night. Karan called on the landline. Mukesh and Gayatri were already asleep as they go to bed quite early. Nandini picked up the phone.

"Where the hell were you? Why is your father calling me at this time of the night constantly? I have told you millions of time that please... for God's sake... use the damn landline for talking at home. Call them now," screamed Karan and cut the call with a bang.

Nandini's heart skipped a beat. Not because of Karan's yelling at her. She was used to it by now. But because she knew that her parents won't usually call at this hour of the night. They sleep quite early. She knew something was wrong. She quickly dialled *baba's* number.

Nandini: Hello? Hello? *Maa... baba... baba?* Hello?

Maa: (crying) "Hello... hello... Nandini... Nandini your *baba... baba* is no more... my child... he left us... he left you... he left me... he—"

Nandini was paralysed for a minute. She couldn't understand what *maa* just said... there was a strange noise, a loud siren that was ringing in her ears... she couldn't hold the receiver and dropped it. After her mind processed the news a bit, she howled and sat on the ground with a thud. This was the news no daughter wants to hear in her life at any point of time.

Listening to her loud cries, both Mukesh and Gayatri came running to her, the call was still going on and Mukesh heard the news from Shashikala. He shared it with Gayatri who was trying her best to console Nandini.

Mukesh tried calling Karan many times but he didn't pick up.

"I don't know when this boy will be back Gayatri. We should leave for Nandini's house. Shashikala *bhabhi* needs us in this tough time. She needs Nandini at all costs," said Mukesh in an anxious voice.

Suddenly, Karan entered the house. Looking at everyone, he got terrified and asked, "What happened? Papa what is going on?"

"You tell me bloody hell where were you? Why are you so late, why were you not picking Nandini's mother's call. Your father-in-law is no more. Nandini's mother was trying to convey that to you since last 1 hour. Where were you?" shouted Mukesh angrily.

"What??... I can't believe this. Papa I was in a meeting. I am so sorry. I... I... am..." replied

Karan. He went to Nandini and kept his hand on Nandini's head consoling her.

"Please calm down, Nandini. Get ready, We are leaving right now. You have to be there with *maa*."

They all left in a rush for Nandini's village. When Nandini reached there, the preparations were going on for *baba's* final rites. Nandini couldn't bear that view. But looking at her *maa* who had fainted, she had to have some courage.

Karan, Mukesh and Gayatri left the next day, leaving Nandini stay behind for some days to be with her mother.

Nandini was still in a huge trauma. *Baba* was suffering from a life-threatening lung disease. This was the reason of his deteriorating health when he went to meet

Nandini on diwali. This was why he was only skull and bones. *Maa* knew about all this. But they both hid it from Nandini because they didn't want her to suffer emotionally.

Nandini was devastated. She couldn't remove any of *baba's* memories that were constantly playing in her mind. His laughter, his care, his love and his voice... all were making Nandini die from inside. This was a kind of pain that was unexplainable for her. She had never faced any pain like this before. Not even when Karan hurts her emotionally or mentally.

No pain...in this entire world... can be as hurtful and unbearable as what she was feeling now — the pain of being separated from a parent... *forever!*

*****

Nandini Returns to *Sasural* With a Heavy Heart

A fortnight later, Mukesh came to take Nandini back home. Nandini was not mentally prepared to leave *maa* all alone and helpless but *maa* wanted her to go with Mukesh. According to her, Nandini's responsibility towards her *sasural* was important. It had been several days since Nandini came home and now *maa* was stable and could take care of herself. It was time for Nandini to get back to her routine life.

"*Bhabhi ji*, I am sorry from Karan's side that he couldn't manage to come. Actually, it was him who was coming today to take Nandini with him but in the last moment, he started feeling really unwell. He had to fix an urgent appointment with the doctor. So, I had to come in his place. Please excuse me," said Mukesh in a low voice.

"Oh, that's absolutely fine Mukesh ji. *Damad ji* must take care if his health. Nandini, you too take care of him, okay. And look after yourself also *beta*," replied Shashikala.

Nandini sat in the back seat of the car. From the back window, she was looking at her *maa's* wrinkled lifeless weak face smiling at her. This time, the separation with *maa* was the hardest. She was standing there all alone. Nandini had never felt this helpless in her entire life... she wanted to stop the car and run to *maa*... and never leave her again. **If only that was possible for a woman!**

It took Nandini several weeks to get back to her normal self. It was a struggle to come back to life after losing *baba*. Indeed, time heals pain... or rather... just makes us get used to live with it.

During this emotionally tough period, one thing that gave Nandini a bit of an inner strength was *maa*.

Day and night, she used to think about how *maa* must be dealing with such a huge loss. *Baba* was *maa's* entire world. She sacrificed all her desires, likes, choices and what not in order to make *baba* her priority. And now when he is not here, the world must seem like hell to her.

Meanwhile, Karan started noticing Nandini's grief and tried behaving good towards her. He would not be rude to her, do all his stuff himself and sometimes, even ask Nandini if she had food. His little attention in this time, proved that he was still a man who was capable of learning empathy. That

there was *hope,* that he was – if nothing more –
a *human!*

*****

Nandini's Regret Rekindles

Nearly three months passed after *baba's* death. Now Nandini calls *maa* often. One evening, she called *maa* from the landline. She decided not to sound a bit worried or emotional for the sake of *maa*. She wanted to be *maa's* strong Nandini. It was *maa* who needed strength more than her.

Nandini: Hello *maa*! How are you?

Maa: (in a weak voice) Hello *beta*, I am good. How is my sweet daughter?

Nandini: I am good too. *Maa* what about your medicines? I hope you are taking them on time. No excuses in that, okay. Remember what doctor said, you have to take medicines daily, no matter if you feel good or bad.

Maa: Yes, my child. I do take them when the blood pressure gets too high.

Nandini: What do you mean *maa*? You have to take them daily without fail. Why are you doing this?

Maa: Oh ho, Nandini. Doctors want people to eat medicines all the time for no reason. It is their job. I am okay my child. And, there are so many things I have to look after with the little money that your *baba* left behind for me dear. I can't waste it simply on unnecessary medicines. I am healthy *beta*. Do not worry about me!

Nandini: *Umm... maa...* do you have sufficient money with you for expense or... I...

Maa: Nandini, you do not have to worry at all my child. I am doing good here. Your *baba* was a considerate man. Do you think he would leave me struggling with money like that? Thing are okay. You take care of yourself.

Nandini: Okay *maa*, take care. I will meet you soon!

After Nandini kept the receiver, her heart sank thinking about the financial struggles her *maa* would be facing. She had an idea that *maa* would only be having a minimal amount of money with her. How will she afford her medicines with that? She has an issue of high blood pressure. The doctor warned her to take a medicine daily on time. But *maa* is not able to take it daily. She is only taking it in the times of emergency when the blood pressure shoots. That was something really risky.

Nandini felt very useless in that hour. She couldn't help her *maa*. She couldn't help *baba* when he was alive. In fact, she can't even help her own self. She was also too scared deep within. Now after losing *baba*, she didn't want to lose *maa*.

Dear diary,

It is not like I didn't feel helpless before for being dependent on people for money. But today, after calling maa, I realised the grave importance of being independent and earning your own money once again. If only I was doing a job and earning money, maa would have been getting the care she needs.

Nobody would have questioned me because it would have been my money. I would have been maa's pillar of strength, her eternal support – like a son, like Karan ji is for mummy ji!

*****

Karan's Unbelievable Betrayal

Dinner was done. Gayatri and Mukesh went to sleep. The weather was not good. It was cloudy and seemed to rain at night. Nandini remembered there were washed clothes on the terrace, left for drying. She quickly went upstairs with an empty bucket to gather the dried clothes. To her surprise, the door of the terrace was already opened. She entered and saw Karan speaking to someone on his phone. Getting a little closer, she could hear him saying...

"Listen to me, Ankita. I am doing my best, okay. Just give me some time. Her father passed just a month back. I can't give her such a shocker at this point of time. Trust me, as soon as she gets recovered from this trauma, I will tell her. I will tell her everything... and I promise... we will be together forever!"

The bucket dropped from Nandini's hand making Karan notice her presence. He turned towards her and his face went pale. He couldn't speak.

Nandini couldn't believe her ears. What was Karan going to tell her? That he was seeing a girl named Ankita, that... he wants to spend his life with her... or that... he was betraying Nandini since the start of her marriage. It has been TWO years... TWO years of them together!

Nandini looked straight into Karan's disloyal eyes to find a trace of shame in them if there was any. Though she didn't utter a single word, her eyes said it all.

She ran downstairs to her room. Locked it and spent the night crying, cursing her life. Little did she know THAT night, was going to be her life-changing night!

Nandini didn't sleep the entire night. How could she? How could any wife? That night, Nandini had to take a decision for her life. Since day 1 of marriage, she had let go of several misunderstandings, multiple insults and plenty of emotional harassments just for the sake of saving her marriage as if it was only one-sided.

From the very start of it, she tried with all her heart and soul to bring things on track with Karan. To keep quiet and have patience for the sake of her parents' respect and esteem. To bear all the pain in this relationship. To attain the badge of being a *good* wife.

BUT ALL WENT IN VAIN!

A wife can bear everything... everything in her marriage but DISLOYALTY!

Now there was no point of surviving in such a hell of a relationship. There was no scope of recovery. All hopes broken. All determination lost.

Nandini's entire married life replayed in her mind like a flop movie. Now she understood why all this indifference, ignorance and dislike towards her from the start. She got answers to all her questions that she once had about Karan's unusual behaviour as a husband.

Nandini felt that it was the time. Time to take a stand for her and her self-esteem. Time to respect her own self worth. Time to...come to a decision that was – *necessary!*

Dear diary,

Tonight seems to be the longest, darkest night for me that would never end if I do not take a decision for myself.

Yes, I am going to take a decision – one that maa would never approve of, one that if baba would have been alive, would never wish it happen.

I am going to cut all my ties with this man whom I call my husband. I no longer wish to be known as his wife. I feel ashamed. I can't see his shameless face and his disloyal eyes any more. I want to be free from this toxic relationship that has always been one-sided.

I don't know what will I do after going to the village but I believe, God give you wings when you work hard for yourself. I will do anything and everything to make my life better.

I deserve better!

*****

Nandini Leaves Karan

It was 5 O'clock in the morning. Nandini packed all her important stuff in one large suitcase, ready to leave – *forever*.

When she went outside in the living room, Mukesh was up. He was reading the newspaper.

"Papa, I am leaving for my house. *Maa* didn't seem to be in her best health on call last week. My heart says I should check on her. *Mummy ji* is sleeping. When she wakes up, please inform her too that I left," said Nandini to Mukesh.

"Suddenly... is everything okay, *beta*? If that is the case then wait, I will come with you to drop," replied Mukesh.

"No, papa. I am good. I will take a bus. Don't worry. I will call you once I reach home," replied Nandini.

"Okay my daughter. Take care and don't forget to inform me once you reach. Give my best wishes to Shashikala *bhabhi*," said Mukesh.

Taking Mukesh's blessings, Nandini left the house.

Mukesh informed Gayatri about this when she woke up. Gayatri got furious. "How can she leave the house without asking me? Why did you let her go like this? What was the emergency? Couldn't she wait for me to wake up?"said Gayatri angrily.

"Gayatri, she must be missing her mother. What happened must be extremely traumatising for her so we have to be gentle with her. Anyway, she will come after some days. She is not going to live there forever. Now calm down," replied Mukesh.

When Gayatri asked Karan about Nandini leaving the house suddenly, he said to her that it was he who advised Nandini to go to her mother for some days as she looked depressed. Gayatri finally calmed down and left for the kitchen without questioning further.

Karan was an opportunist. He quickly understood the things and played it really well to hide his betrayal from his parents.

*****

Nandini Reaches Home

The bus dropped Nandini at the stop near her house. She walked her way from there. For some strange reason, Nandini was feeling free for the first time after so long. This feeling of freedom was similar to the one that she had before marriage — when she was a young unmarried girl, returning from her school.

Unexpectedly, Nandini was happier than usual.

She saw *maa* watering the plants in the small area at the main gate of the house.

As soon as she saw that familiar view of her house, *baba's* strong recollection of memories engulfed her mind. She stopped there for a minute. Standing afar from the house, just trying to capture how it used to be when *baba* was alive.

She remembered her childhood self running with *maa's* purse to buy an ice-cream on hearing the tingling sound made by the ice-cream seller.

Baba would catch her in time and laugh at her mischief. Then he would buy it for both his wife and daughter.

Those clips from her childhood shook her to the core. They appeared to be as fresh and real as yesterday. Suddenly, she heard *maa* coughing a lot and with that, she returned to her present.

She went closer to *maa* and hugged her from behind. Shashikala was startled at first but when she turned around to see who it was, she was delighted.

"Oh my dear lord! My daughter is here. How are you?" asked Shashikala.

"*Maa*, how do I look? All good, right? You tell me, how is your health?" replied Nandini.

"Now it will be perfect. Come, lets go inside," said Shashikala.

Both of them went inside and were having a lot of gossips full of love when Shashikala realised that Nandini came all alone for the first time like this. This made her question things.

She asked Nandini, "Why did you come alone, Nandini? Where is *damad ji* or *bhaisahab?* Is everything okay at home?"

"*Maa*, actually Karan ji has gone out of country for about six months on his office tour. As I was missing you so much, he said that by the time he returns home, I can spend my time with you. He was too worried about you, *maa*. And papa was not well."

"So, I came alone taking a bus. Now I can be with my lovely *maa* for a good period of time," replied Nandini.

"That's wonderful. But do keep calling *damad ji* and asking about his well-being. Do not forget about him totally, okay," said *maa*.

"Yeah *maa*. I know you love your *damad ji* more than me, I am jealous... hahaha," replied Nandini.

Nandini was very good at convincing Shashikala about how perfect her married life was. That's what she has been doing since day 1 of her marriage. She never said the truth and the reason is pretty obvious that she didn't want her parents to feel sad, worried or scared for their daughter's future.

*****

Karan's Plan

Fifteen days later, Mukesh asked Gayatri to call Shashikala and ask about Nandini's return to home. Gayatri was still mad at Nandini for leaving the house without her permission.

She replied, "Not at all. Why would I ask her anything? She left all of a sudden without telling me. Now let her come back the way she had left. All by herself."

At night, on the dinner table, Mukesh asked Karan about the same thing. "Papa, actually I told Nandini that it has been two years of our marriage and she had never been able to spend much time with her parents since then. Now that her maa is alone, she should spend a good period of time with her. So, let her be there for a month and then I'll bring her back." replied Karan.

Both Mukesh and Gayatri felt something abnormal and strange about Karan's answer but they didn't say anything because it was a matter between a husband and his wife.

Karan was glad that this happened without him doing anything. It was a golden opportunity for him as Nandini had left the house herself without making any fuss about his disloyalty.

He wanted to grab this chance from so long. Now that his way was clear, he thought that it was the perfect time for him to introduce Ankita to his parents.

*****

Ankita

Ankita was the bank manager in the same bank where Karan was an executive. However, Ankita was not just any other colleague. Her father was the Chief Bank Officer. She came from a high class, rich background. Her family was one of the famous ones in the city.

Karan always wanted to marry Ankita. However, the reason behind that was a little selfish. He wanted to be promoted to a senior position in his bank. This is why he kept on luring Ankita from the last three years.

Initially, he had no hopes because of their 'poles apart' societal status. So, having no way out, he married Nandini. But recently, Ankita too started noticing him as well. They both started spending time together. So much so that whenever Karan said that he would be late from office, the reason was that he would take Ankita out for dinners.

This was the same reason why he stopped giving the full amount of salary at home; in order to pay Ankita's expensive dinner and shopping bills.

Karan knew Ankita won't go with any random local guy. So, he pretended to be a good match to her by telling her stories of his lavish lifestyle.

Poor Ankita got trapped in his emotional forgery. But this did not go well for long. Ankita was asking Karan to meet his parents. She knew everything about Karan's marriage but as usual he created false stories of how he only did it under pressure for his ailing mother.

Karan was waiting for the right time to

break the news to Nandini and throw her back to her house after which he would let his parents know about him and Ankita.

But since he was a cunning man, he planned it to go slowly. He didn't want to rush anything or state it all at once. He knew that his parents won't approve it that easily. So, he wanted to take things slow.

*****

Nandini's Cooking Classes

It had been quite a few days since Nandini came to her house. She noticed that there was hardly any money left with *maa*. On top of her own expense, now *maa* had to bear Nandini's expense too. This made Nandini think hard about how could she support *maa*?

After contemplating a lot, Nandini realised that not all jobs require a college degree. Some are based just on skills and knowledge. It was a legit fact that Nandini was brilliant in cooking. She thought, what if she starts taking cooking classes? That needs no interviews or certificates.

Nandini made a big hoarding from the left over cardboards in *baba's* attic. On it, she wrote **'Nandini's Cooking Classes'** and hanged it from the top of her front-facing terrace wall.

She set the fees very minimal because

she knew that the girls in the village couldn't afford much and won't be able to join if it is high. Soon, people started enquiring about her classes.

Listening about the low fee, there was a good number of girls who wanted to join it.

*****

Ankita Comes Over for Dinner

Karan thought that it was a good idea to invite Ankita over for a dinner now that Nandini was not there.

"Mummy, papa, actually tomorrow there is a guest coming over for dinner with us. Her name is Ankita. She is my bank manager. Mummy, make sure the preparations are good. Make 3-4 dishes and a dessert too. This is important for my promotion," informed Karan to his parents on the dining table.

As this dinner was necessary for Karan's promotion at bank, Gayatri left no stone unturned to make it a perfect feast.

There was long list of items. From *shahi paneer* to *dal makhani* and *gulab jamun* for dessert, the dinner spread looked tempting. Soft drinks were also the part of the feast.

Quite ironically, Gayatri who was too old and weak to help Nandini in the kitchen even for special occasions like diwali, prepared all of this alone and that too with an unmatched energy.

Greed ran in the family blood!

Table was set and the mother-son duo was waiting for the special guest to arrive. Karan got a message on phone from Ankita saying she was there on the start of the street, with her driver struggling to park the SUV anywhere.

Karan went to escort her. He made the driver park the car in a ground at a little distance from the street. Ankita had to walk to his home for about 10 minutes.

Ankita and Karan reached the latter's house with Ankita all sweaty and weary from walking in the humid weather.

"Welcome *beta*, come inside," said Gayatri to Ankita very lovingly.

"Hello aunty, how are you?" asked Ankita.

"Oh, we are good. It must be tough for you to find our house, isn't it?" asked Gayatri.

"Don't ask me aunty, it was horrible. Even the GPS was struggling to show this narrow street. Took me an hour to find. Plus, there is no parking space for cars here," Ankita replied.

Gayatri felt weird for a second listening to Ankita's unfiltered reply but never minded. They all went into the living room.

Ankita turned speechless when she took a look at Karan's house. Actually, she was already pissed from the start of the street but still had hopes due to Karan's bragging of a lavish lifestyle.

However, when she sat in the living room, she looked at each bit of it very specifically. She judged every single thing of the house. The old-style structure, the paint-chipped walls, the weary furniture, the small size of it... every single thing... as she had a quite different version of it in her mind.

"Can you please turn on the AC Karan? Its so hot in here," asked Ankita.

"We don't have an AC in the living room. We only have them in our bedrooms," replied Karan.

"Take her to our room Karan. Make her comfortable. She must be feeling uneasy *beta*," suggested Gayatri but Ankita denied saying its fine.

After having a small session of conversation, Gayatri invited Ankita to the dinner table. Karan called Mukesh too to have dinner and meet Ankita.

"How are you Ms. Ankita?" asked Mukesh

"I am good uncle. Please join us for the dinner," replied Ankita.

When Gayatri started removing the lids from the casseroles, Ankita made a remark that made everyone present uncomfortable.

"Oh my goodness! Aunty, don't mind but you all take such an unhealthy diet. That's a lot of oil. Karan, look at you, that is from where you are getting all that fat. Hahaha."

Gayatri wasn't really happy with her demeaning reply but still carried on serving the food in Ankita's plate herself.

"Ankita *beta*, you tell me, what do you eat? Next time, I will cook the same thing for you like your mother does, okay?" said Gayatri sportingly.

"Aunty, mom doesn't cook. We have a helping staff for all the household chores. To be honest, we seldom eat together. Mom barely gets time from her fashion designing work and dad is always busy. Sometimes... I wish I could enjoy these little things like a middle-class family of yours," replied Ankita.

Karan didn't like Ankita's rude comments. His face said it all.

Mukesh got so uncomfortable at her constant remarks that made them feel inferior. Suddenly, he choked on his food and started coughing. Karan and Gayatri gave him water and patted his back rigorously.

But looking at Mukesh coughing at the dining table, Ankita got annoyed and kept her hand at her mouth. She instantly stopped eating and drank some water.

"You have eaten so less Ankita. Take some more of it," said Gayatri.

"No, I am done aunty. Ah... Karan, I think I should leave now. It's getting late," said Ankita.

"Okay sure. I'll drop you to your car," replied Karan.

Ankita stood up, all set to leave Karan's house when Gayatri told her to wait for a second. She went to her room and came back with an envelope of money.

"Here, take this my dear. This is the first time that you have come to our house.

Do return soon, okay," said Gayatri.

"What is this thing aunty?" asked Ankita with a curiosity. She took the envelope and opened it then and there itself.

When she saw a 500-rupee note in it, she laughed and said, "Aunty, you do not need to do this formality. This doesn't happen in my society. In fact, we don't even give these petty things to our staff. You keep it. It's okay. And thanks for the dinner."

Both Gayatri and Mukesh felt ashamed and belittled to the core. Karan couldn't digest his parents' disrespect and that too from the woman who was going to be a part of his family – *according to him.*

*****

Ankita's Outrage

When Ankita went out of the gate, he grabbed her arm and said, "What's wrong with you Ankita? How dare you belittle my parents? I noticed that from the moment you stepped in... I didn't expect this from you... you have —" Ankita stopped him in between and removed his hand with a force and replied with a rage.

"Shut up... just shut your deceitful mouth up. What did you say? You didn't expect this from me, right? And what about you? What did you do to me all this while? Pretended to be a different 'Karan' I knew."

"You showed me the things that never existed. You bloody liar, a fraudster, you lied about your lavish lifestyle, your like-dislikes, your extravagant choices... just to impress me. You knew it very well that if I knew your middle-class status, you won't stand a chance to even be my friend, let alone my love interest."

Listening to the chaos, Mukesh and Gayatri went out of the house and stood seeing the drama happening between Karan and Ankita.

"Ankita, I know my way could be wrong but my intention was pure. I... I wanted to know you... I wanted to spend my life with a person like you... I... ," replied Karan.

"You wanted to spend your life with me? Oh! really? No... you wanted to spend your life with a successful daughter of a successful father, Karan. I was only your key to promotion. That's it. And I was such a fool that I trusted a betrayer like you. I should have understood that a cheap man like you who can leave his wife for 'another girl', can any day leave that 'another girl' too for a better option," said Ankita in an uncontrollable anger.

"Ankita... listen to me. Calm down. We will sit and talk about this properly... I promise —" pleaded Karan.

"No! You listen to me. If you ever try to come near me or contact me now, I swear you will spend the rest of your life in jail. Remember, who am I. Not your naive, mute wife whom you played for two years, okay,"

"And yes, you wanted to get promoted via playing with my emotions, right? Now, I will make sure you are fired from the job. That's the least you deserve," yelled Ankita and left in anger.

Karan couldn't accept what just happened. All his plans, male ego, self-esteem were crushed by Ankita. And he couldn't do anything in return – *anything at all.*

He was so helpless in that moment.

A failed man without a wife, without a relationship and now... without a job too.

His parents now finally knew the reason behind Nandini's sudden exit from the house. They understood that not only did Karan lie to Ankita but also to them about Nandini and her reason to leave for the village.

They were disappointed!

Mukesh was ashamed of his degree-holder son who was once his pride. Gayatri felt pathetic for every bad behaviour that she had shown towards her daughter-in-law Nandini. Now she realised that Nandini was a real gem of a girl. The way Ankita demeaned them, made her realise the value they held in Nandini's eyes.

Gayatri couldn't sleep that night. She regretted every act of dishonour and spite against Nandini. She wished Nandini to come back to the house but she couldn't ask her that due to her son's grave mistake.

*****

Nandini's First Earning

Nandini was trying harder each day to make it for *maa*. She was doing more than her capability.

Nandini was such a polite and soft-spoken human which proved as a demerit for her relationship. But contrary to that, this time, it became her *USP*. Girls were so happy that no matter how many mistakes they made while learning the dishes, their teacher would help them through again and again without screaming at them or demeaning them.

Suddenly, **'Nandini's Cooking Classes'** became a house hold name. Nearly all the girls from her village got enrolled into it. In fact, some of her students used to come from neighbouring villages as well.

Since Nandini was also good in sewing and

embroidering, she started taking orders for making dresses and that too for a reasonable rate.

Indeed, talent is never necessitous of a degree.

After the struggle of a month, it was time for her to receive her first income. **When she got the money from her students, she tied it into the *pallu* of her saree. That moment gave her a completely new feeling which she never experienced before... in that moment... she felt— powerful!**

Gradually, Nandini started earning adequate money collectively from all the services she offered. She was so happy to be able to do that. After providing everything for *maa,* she used that money to buy the thing that she used to rely on others for – *a smart phone.*

Nandini and *maa* were extremely excited on

the former's achievement. However, *maa* was always sure that Nandini was a knowledgeable girl as she was good at household chores but she didn't expect Nandini to turn her skills into money.

But *maa* was also worried. She asked Nandini if Karan calls her? To which Nandini replied, "*Maa*, of course he does. It's not possible for him to call daily from there but... he does it often when he gets time,"

"Okay, so next time he calls, make me talk to him too. It has been so many days since I heard his voice," replied *maa*.

Nandini was tensed. She didn't know for how long she had to lie to *maa* about her broken married life. She even gave it a thought multiple times if she should just tell *maa* everything and finish this for life. But each time she remembered that *maa* won't be able to live with it. So, she decided to keep going as long as she could... and as long as *maa* is convinced.

*****

Nandini's New Smartphone

Finally, her wait was over when there was a package delivered at her door. It was her brand new self-purchased first touch-screen smart phone. Nandini was on cloud nine that day. Luckily, it was Sunday and her classes were off. So, she spent her entire day knowing her phone, its features, the ways she could use it for her work and most importantly, knowing what is social media and its influence on one's work.

She googled it all and saw several tips available on the websites to help her increase her reach. Then she discovered the game changer for her classes – *Youtube.*

She saw how people were using youtube to upload videos of cooking and earning in millions. Nandini got an idea from it. Since it was free to make use of it, Nandini created an account on youtube with the same name **'Nandini**'s **Cooking Classes'**.

She started live recording her cooking classes with her phone and then uploaded them raw on youtube without any editing.

Initially, Nandini didn't know anything about editing so her videos didn't get many views as they were way too long. But soon, she was able to learn good video editing too. Some information about it she got from her students who were tech-savvy and wanted their hard working teacher to succeed in the field while some on her own.

*****

Karan's Downfall

After Ankita got Karan fired by her father, he was struggling to find a job in the banking sector again. Ankita and her father had big influential terms with people at higher positions.

Karan spent his days and nights searching for a job. He was tensed as he had old parents to feed at home. He was feeling helpless. Just like Nandini did when she was dependent on Karan.

Remember how she used to die inside thinking of her ailing mother who got nothing left after *baba's* death. Karan was feeling the same way for his parents now.

Mukesh and Gayatri stopped paying attention towards Karan because of what he did with Nandini and what he further planned to do.

Although Gayatri was a greedy lady, she didn't know that Karan was planning to get married to Ankita. She just thought that Ankita was Karan's senior, so he needed to butter her for promotion.

That is why she was serving Ankita hard. But she never wanted anything like this to happen... to leave Nandini in the middle of nowhere, to lie to someone's daughter just for some money, and to hide such a big thing from parents.

Gayatri thought to call Shashikala many times, but each time she stopped herself thinking that by then, Shashikala would have known about Karan's grave betrayal and thus, how can she face Shashikala being a mother herself?

Since parents didn't talk to Karan any more, he was left all alone. He got isolated just as Nandini was in his house. The room that once felt lifeless, suffocating and silent to Nandini, now felt the same for Karan.

It was a uno-reverse. Now, Karan was at Nandini's place, emotionally and mentally. He could feel all that Nandini once felt with him. However, he only felt 50% per cent of it but was already struggling to continue in that phase of life.

*****

Karan's Growing Realisation Of Nandini's Goodness

Five months passed since Nandini left the house. Karan was depressed. Somewhere he knew that why was all of that happening to him? Why was he not getting a simple job anywhere? Why his parents were suffering due to his fault? Why... his life took a 360 degree turn? He knew the answer to it but it took him 5 months to accept that.

Karan knew how was he with Nandini even when she was the only person in his life who was ready to be with him for no profit... *in fact she always ended up in loss with him.*

After Ankita left him, he compared her with Nandini and found that she was nowhere even half as good as Nandini. May be because

Ankita was an independent girl who gave Karan the taste of his own medicine.

However, he did feel how Nandini would respect him and his parents, how she would serve Karan like a deity even after his ruthless behaviour, and how she would never complaint about anything.

That day when Nandini found out about Karan's betrayal, she could have easily created a big-time chaos in the house. She could have downgraded his parents too or could have demanded a divorce and alimony to compensate. But she did nothing of that sort.

She just walked away... *silently*.

They say... **it is better if a person you do wrong with, argues back — because if he doesn't... then you have to pay the price of his silence your entire life.**

When a hurtful person leaves his case in God's hands, God makes sure to give it back to the person who hurt him – *quite strongly!*

Karan could sense that happening to him. He became quite and endured the pain just like Nandini did. He was wanting to run away from his toxic life but couldn't. He needed to continue, for the sake of his parents. Again... just like Nandini did.

One night, one of Karan's friend called him and said that there was a job for him but not in the banking sector. He would get lesser salary as compared to his previous job but still, something is better than nothing.

Karan agreed.

He ironed his formal shirt, gathered his important files and set an alarm for the morning next day for the interview.

The only thing left to keep in his office bag was the print-out of his CV that he brought in the morning. He wasn't sure where did he keep it. He searched for it everywhere in the room. When he checked the last drawer of the bedside table, he found it. But along with it, he also found a diary.

*****

Karan Finds Nandini's Diary

It was an unfamiliar diary. It was not his of course. It was the first time he was seeing that diary. He opened it and turned some pages. The writing was different too. He didn't understand whom it belonged to. It looked as if it was someone's journal. So, he read a few pages to know who it was about.

When he read the first page of it, he felt like the world stopped. It felt strange. He knew who was it – *Nandini*. He was happy and sad at the same time. Happy to find something linked to her, sad to remember that she is not with him any more.

He forgot about all his interview preparations. Instead, he started reading Nandini's diary from the very first page. The more he read, the more he hated himself.

But still, he spent the entire night reading every single word of it.

The truthfulness, the innocence and the insecurity with which Nandini had written each word, made him tremble with regret.

The diary did to him what Nandini couldn't. He finally got to know who Nandini was due to her diary. Her maturity, her patience, her unspoken words... were all encased in her diary.

Karan Gets to Know Nandini As The Unheard Housewife

The diary told Karan that Nandini was – the unheard housewife.

She was never heard, never valued, never understood... never *loved* as a wife while she deserved the world. She deserved the sky.

Karan was devastated to know how she never wanted to marry early, how she wanted to study instead, how she grew likeness for Karan, how she sacrificed her desires, likes and choices for him and how badly she wanted him to act like a *normal husband*.

But for some reason, the entire diary was different than the last page of it. Throughout her diary, she wrote about hopes, determination and perseverance to make her marriage work out.

All the pages wanted to give Karan second chances one after one to correct himself. However, the last page was the end of all of it.

Karan read that last page with a heavy heart. The page got wet with his tears all over. He read about how Nandini was forced to cut her ties with him. How she felt while writing this last page after being so positive and hopeful all these two years of marriage.

She was in such a painful place herself emotionally but she never complained... never said anything. Or maybe she tried to say... but she was always left unheard.

Karan couldn't breathe and felt a pang of pain in his chest. This pain represented that Karan was doomed. Doomed to lose a wife like Nandini.

*****

Karan's Repentance

Karan realised that he horribly failed as a husband, a son-in-law, a son, but more so ever... *a human.*

He failed to give physical, emotional or financial security to Nandini. He failed to be her life-partner.

Karan was twisting and tossing in this invisible pain. This pain was not physical which he could easily endure. This pain was deep inside his heart.

Finally, Karan couldn't bear and decided to ask for an apology to Nandini. He knew that Nandini would never want to see his fraudulent face again but he wanted to give it one last try. Anyway, Karan had a hope to meet her as they were not yet legally separated.

Nandini just left the house and decided not to come back ever. But legally, they were still married.

So, Karan decided that he would go to her house and just ask for one thing – forgiveness, if possible.

Even if that means to give Nandini the legal freedom from this toxic marriage, he was ready to do so for her happiness. He was ready to step out of her life as he was like a blood-sucking parasite to her emotionally.

His conscience needed to make that apology in order to sustain!

He didn't sleep for the entire night and was waiting for the sun to rise impatiently.

Around 5.17 am in the morning, he didn't wait to take a bus or a taxi. Instead, he took his bullet and left for Nandini's village without telling anything to anyone.

*****

Nandini's Journey: From Ashes to Wings

Nandini worked hard to balance all the things she was doing to earn money at the same time. Her need turned into her passion. She was enjoying her growth, financial independence and hustle.

All her efforts and success made her really confident and made her feel *alive*. She left Karan's house thinking it to be the end of her life but now, she was having the best time of her life miraculously.

From a voiceless, weak and terrified Nandini, She was turned into a courageous, strong and a brave Nandini.

Nandini's youtube channel was a very promising one. Though it started slow, within a span of just four months with Nandini's hard work of day and night, it grew to 2k subscribers. Her students were happier than her for her success. They too contributed majorly in the journey because she treated all of them like her family.

When Nandini's channel had hit 2k subscribers, her students decided to celebrate it. They told Nandini to be ready the following day to have a blast.

*****

The Unexpected Guest

It was the time for Nandini's cooking classes to begin. The door bell rang. Nandini thought that the students were all there, ready to barge in with beaming smiles. She excitedly ran towards the door and opened it.

Her facial expressions turned from excitement to a shock. She wasn't ready to see what she saw at the door. *It was Karan!*

He was standing in front of Nandini in unruly hair and beard, swollen eyes with dark under-bags beneath and messy clothes. It seemed as if it was not Karan, *but a homeless, depressed man!*

In his hands were two packets of something. They appeared to be from a sweet shop.

Nandini was blank. She couldn't react.

She was standing there, looking at Karan like a strange thing. She was speechless. She was struck by the lightening of all the memories of her past spent with this man. *The bad, the worse, the ugly.*

"Who is at the door Nandini?" asked *maa*.

(silence)

"Who is there, Nandini?" asked *maa* again.

When Nandini didn't answer for long, *maa* went to check on her.

"Oh! *damad ji?* What a pleasant surprise! I am seeing you after such a long time. Nandini, why is he still standing at the door? Come inside quickly my child, I am so happy to see you." said *maa* excitedly.

Karan was shocked to see that loving

behaviour of Shashikala towards him. He expected the worse as he thought that Nandini would have told her *maa* about everything that happened.

He entered the house and touched Shashikala's feet. He then gave her the two packets that he held in his hands.

"This is for you and Nandini, *maa*," said Karan hesitatingly.

"My dear son, how are you? When did you come back from *vilayat*? I missed you so much but I have a complaint... why you didn't call your maa even once? Didn't you miss me too? I know... you only missed just one woman – your wife Nandini, hahaha," said Shashikala lovingly.

Now, Karan got it why Shashikala said that. Nandini didn't tell anything to her mother. And after knowing Nandini as a person through her diary, he also knew the reason behind it.

Shashikala made him sit on the sofa and asked him about everything. From his parents to his work. She also asked him about his well-being as he looked really unhealthy.

Meanwhile, Nandini was standing afar and looking at both of them – still speechless.

"Nandini, why are your standing there, *beta*. Your husband has come after so long. Don't be shy like a new bride now. Come here. Both of you sit and talk while I make some snacks for you," said Shashikala and left them alone.

Both of them sat there like a piece of meat. None of them had courage to speak. One out of guilt and the other... out of lack of words.

Shashikala returned back quickly with refreshments and asked Nandini to take Karan to her room as he looked pretty tired from the journey.

"Nandini, take *damad ji* to your room so that he can have some rest. He looks quite exhausted. After a little nap he'll feel better, right," said Shashikala looking at Karan.

They both went into the room. Karan sat on the bed while Nandini kept standing at the door which she locked to avoid *maa* from hearing anything. She was assuming Karan to ask her for a – *divorce*.

*****

Nandini Breaks Down

"H-How.... are... you... Nandini?" asked Karan with a tone of shame and guilt in his voice.

In her reply, Nandini just slightly nodded her head. She was in a habit of nodding head when she felt that there is no use of speaking anything.

"*Hmm...* I was... just... thinking about you. It has been... five months since you... left," said Karan further.

It took some time for Nandini to get back to her senses after seeing Karan all of a sudden but when she got the hang of it, she was confident to ask his reason for being at her door.

"What do you want from me now?

An official divorce? Have you also brought in the papers?" asked Nandini in a trembling voice.

"No... No... not at all... I ... I just came to... see you —" replied Karan.

"What did you want to see? If the wounds that you have given me have healed or not? Or to see if I am dead or alive from all the unimaginable pain that you have given to my heart? What did you want to see?" replied Nandini with all her inner strength.

"No... please... listen to me once... for God's sake... I... I... am not here to... to hurt you again... I wanted to meet you and..." said Karan but was cut short by Nandini.

"But I don't want to see you any more, ever again. I... I just don't even want to waste my time telling you that how I felt like dying that day... how I felt as if I can't breathe that day... how... how it was all over for me... that bloody day when you... when you decided to abandon me in the middle of nowhere... when I lost *baba*... when I needed you the most... you left me all alone... then what the hell do you want to see me now for?" asked Nandini crying like a child.

"Nandini, please listen to me... I am here just to... to apologize for everything... everything that I did to you... you didn't deserve any bit of it... listen to me once... then I will leave forever if you wish —"replied Karan

"Apologize?? Can your few words of apology bring my excitement that I had while getting married to you back? Can it bring my first wedding night back? Can it bring my first diwali back? Can it bring my dreams, my desires, my hopes and my...my two years of struggling to survive my marriage back? Can it bring my self-respect, my worth as a wife and value as a human in your eyes back? Can it?? NO! None of it can bring back the time gone......" sat Nandini on the bed opposite to Karan, crying profusely this time.

"I think you should leave right now, just leave me... for once and all and end this continuous pain. Please... I beg you," continued Nandini, folding her hands to plead Karan.

Karan was shattered to see Nandini in such a vulnerable phase all due to him. He went towards her and sat down on his knees at Nandini's feet.

"Nandini, please... for one last time... let me say it all out. I will die if I leave from here without asking your forgiveness... please let me apologize... please... then the choice will be in your hands... to forgive me or not... but please... give me a chance to do it... please!" begged Karan.

He wanted to hold Nandini's shaking hands and wipe her tears but he knew she won't allow him to touch her.

So, to calm her down, he stood up and filled the glass with water kept at the table in the room. He gave it to Nandini which she denied first but after his continuous pleading, took it and drank some of it.

Karan then sat down again on his knees at Nandini's feet. Now that she was a little better, he wanted to confess to her, his faults and his regret.

*****

Karan's Apology

Karan opened up his heart to Nandini...

"Nandini... It is true that I never wanted to marry you... ever. I had different plans in my life – different goals. I wanted to achieve an unimaginable success in life. I thought I needed a woman with a similar aspirations beside me, not the one who was only limited to the four walls of a house."

"I always felt that I didn't get what I deserved as a partner. But I was such a big fool Nandini, I was such a big fool!"

"I got so obsessed with this thought of mine that you are not my type that I didn't even realise where I was leading to... I didn't understand what I was doing to a human, a wife — my wife."

"I am ashamed to admit that I failed – failed as a husband, as a son-in-law and even as a human too!"

"I am ashamed to accept that I ruined everything that was so special for you. Our wedding night, your wedding gift, your first diwali, your special rituals, events, parties... every damn thing."

"I ruined our marriage which had always been one-sidedly run by you. I ruined your desires, your dreams... I... I ruined everything Nan — Nandini."

Saying this, Karan broke down in tears. Nandini still couldn't see him this helpless and weak. She wanted to console him but... something inside her was so broken, that didn't allow her to make that move.

Karan continued, "Nandini, I know the kind of person you are, you can forgive me for all these mistakes that I did, for all the times I broke your heart with my ignorance, but can you forgive me for my sin too? I cheated you when you needed me the most, when your *baba* died... when... you were searching for him in me... I am a bloody betrayer who left you alone for a person who never wanted me... for whom I was nothing because of my low status. I left you only because I wanted to achieve a higher status in life... stepping on someone else's shoulder."

"You can forgive me for my faults but can you forgive me for my sin, Nandini? Can you? No, never... and I deserve this. I deserve all the sufferings that I made you go through."

"This is the last time you are seeing this cheater Nandini. I can't look into your eyes ever again. I wanted – I wanted to confess that when you left and life kicked me back, it opened my eyes."

"Your departure from my life... taught me what I lost. I lost the person for whom I was the entire world, I lost the most important relation of my life. And with that, I lost my self-esteem, my courage, my feelings and my dignity too... Nandini."

Nandini was listening to each word coming out of Karan's mouth with naked truthfulness. This is the longest Karan had ever talked to her. Although she didn't want to listen to him furthermore, the broken girl inside her was healing due to his acceptance and repentance – *word by word.*

"Nandini, I know that now nothing can change what I had done to you, and nothing can bring back those two years of our toxic marriage... but I... I am here to ask for your forgiveness. I am sorry... I am so so sorry Nandini."

"I am sorry for making your feel inferior, for snatching all your wife rights, for never fulfilling any of your responsibilities, your desires, your hidden dreams... nothing. For never giving you the value that you deserved as my wife, for always making you feel sad, invisible, unattended and unheard!"

"I am sorry... I really am Nandini."

"I... I... don't know if it makes any sense now but... I love you Nandini. I don't know how will I survive with this baggage of losing the love of my life... and hurting her the most. Of knowing that she is not there in my life any more... and she would never return!"

Karan couldn't continue and begged Nandini to forgive him with both hands folded together. Tears running down his eyes as a proof of his regret and helplessness.

The room was filled with an awkward silence between Nandini and Karan but also with a sea of emotions of all kinds.

Karan felt lighter after speaking his heart out to Nandini. He said it all, out loud. As he was gathering some courage to look into Nandini's eyes for the last time before leaving, he still had an undying hope that maybe Nandini would forgive him.

For a good five minutes, Karan kept looking into Nandini's eyes to find his answer, but they were looking somewhere else.

Perhaps, Karan got his answer. It was a NO!

With a heavy heart, he stood up, turned towards the door of the room and walked

away when he heard Nandini saying,
" Wait..."

*****

Nandini's Answer

After a short pause, Nandini continued, "Once again, you are leaving me unheard like you always did. Nothing has changed in you."

Karan turned around and looked at Nandini.

"You asked me for forgiveness but you're leaving without knowing my answer... again... as if my opinion still doesn't matter... as if I am still invisible to you," said Nandini.

Karan replied, "No, its not like that Nandini. I waited for your answer and you didn't say anything. Plus, I could read your eyes which were not ready to forg—"

"Oh! keep quiet. Only if you were too good at reading eyes, this day would have never come for us," replied Nandini.

Karan started moving towards her when she stopped him and told him to stay standing at his place.

"Don't come near me. I am not ready to be broken again by you. The old crack in my heart is still unfilled. The wound from loving you is still so green. Don't do this to me again. I know, I know that you will hurt me again if I – I forgive you," said Nandini in a hurtful voice.

"No. Nandini. I will never hurt you again. I promise. I will leave you and never come back. Trust me, I will never show you my unfaithful self again, ever. Please forgive me for one last time!" replied Karan.

"So, you confessed your love only to leave me again? In the middle... to myself... forever? All these emotions, regret and repentance for never meeting again? And it is only you who decides what should be done? Again... like always, without knowing my consent?" asked Nandini.

Karan stood at his place confused like a lost person. He couldn't understand what Nandini meant. He seemed so distressed at decoding Nandini's emotions.

Nandini walked closer to Karan and said...

"You know what *maa* says? It is very easy to break a relation but it takes years of hard work and millions of sacrifices to make one. A successful marriage requires falling in love multiple times, with the same person. It is a union of two imperfect people tied together for eternity."

"So, to make or break a marriage is in the hands of only those two people. It is a commitment till death. If they wish, they can leave any time, but if don't, they can go to any limits to make it work. *Baba* always taught me that when life gives you a second chance or if a person who wrongs you, returns to you with a heart full of regret and arms open asking for forgiveness... go for it before its too late."

"Today, my married life has given me a second chance. A chance to correct it and start all over again. To be someone's wife again, to fall in love again! And this time, I won't lose my right like a mute weak woman that I was. I will grab it hard and make sure you don't leave in the middle – again!"

Nandini's words left Karan in a huge shock. This was the last thing he expected from her. Not only did Nandini forgive him but also wanted to accept his companionship for the second time.

Karan went crazy and hugged Nandini

like a child. He couldn't believe his ears and asked Nandini to spend her life with him again. But this time, like a proper proposal, bending down on one knee.

Wanting to change Nandini's mood, he playfully asked her, *"Umm...* So, Mrs Karan... are you ready to spend the rest of your life with me?"

"Yes", replied Nandini like the same old excited bride who had dreams in her eyes for her new journey.

They both felt like their happiest self that day after a long... long time of emotional distress.

"Nandini, I will make sure you get all the happiness of this world. You deserve it all. My life... my wife!" said Karan passionately.

He asked Nandini to pack her bags as they would leave for their house the next day. It had been so many months of their separation and Karan wanted to surprise his parents too who were dying to see Nandini back in the house as their *bahu*.

"But... *maa* is all alone here and... I don't want to leave her alone any more in this age," replied Nandini.

"Just give me some time Nandini, and soon I will do something about it too. We will take *maa* with us forever," said Karan.

Nandini got happy to see Karan's change towards her mother as well.

She quickly packed her bag and told *maa* that she would return soon to be with her and this time with a surprise.

*****

The Couple Was Set to Go Home

The next morning, Nandini informed all her students that they could continue learning cooking through her youtube channel. And she would keep taking trips to the village for some special classes too.

Karan, Nandini and *maa* were done with the breakfast. Nandini was all set to leave with Karan, who was waiting outside on his bullet, looking at the hoarding **'Nandini's Cooking Classes.'**

Nandini had told Karan all about her achievements the previous night. How she worked day and night to get it and how her students helped her immensely in finding the way to success.

While Karan was ashamed to listen how she had to struggle after he abandoned her, he was really proud of her at the same time.

She also showed Karan her youtube channel. Karan was amazed looking at Nandini's growth — *both personal and professional.*

She was a totally different person. It was something that Karan always wanted to have in his life partner – *self confidence.*

After meeting *maa,* the couple left for the city. On their way, Karan asked Nandini if she would like to have some snacks at a local café. They stopped for a while for a break and spent some quality time together.

They finally reached home after nearly 1.5 hours of travel. Karan kept on rigorously ringing the bell of the main door of his house.

He was dying to tell mummy and papa that their daughter-in-law was back.

"Coming... wait, who rings the bell continuously like this?" said Gayatri annoyed by it.

As soon as she opened the door, all her irritation vanished when saw Nandini standing along with Karan.

She immediately hugged her and started crying.

Nandini hugged her back.

"Mummy lets go inside and cry, otherwise the entire street will join you in this," said Karan jokingly.

"Papa, where are you? Look who is here? Your *bahu*," said Karan searching for Mukesh.

Mukesh came out from the bedroom listening to Karan. He got extremely ecstatic to see Nandini back in the house. She came towards him and touched his feet. Mukesh was overwhelmed.

Both Gayatri and Mukesh were too happy that didn't ask anything about what and why it happened. They just welcomed Nandini with open arms. After a long time, there was a moment of love and togetherness in their house.

*****

Nandini Continued Her Classes

That night, Nandini got to know that Karan lost his job and was on a job hunt. Due to which, it was difficult to run the house on his savings which was slowly getting diminished.

"Don't worry. I am with you. By the time you get a good job, I will take care of all the household expenses. Now I can do that. I am getting a good return from my youtube channel and I am also thinking to continue taking my cooking classes here," said Nandini to Karan holding his hand in hers.

Soon, Karan set up the hoarding of **'Nandini's Cooking Classes'** on his house. As she had a growing community over youtube, some people already knew her from her videos. So, she got a good response quickly without struggling much.

She started her classes in full motion and continued uploading videos. She bore all her family expenses and of *maa's* too.

Meanwhile, Karan got a job. It was not as good as the previous one but not too bad either. After some time, their family got back on track financially.

Karan told Nandini that he wants to get the first floor of the house constructed so that they could move upstairs and then he would bring in *maa* who could be shifted to their old room on the ground floor.

Anyway, they needed more space now in order to run Nandini's cooking classes as the number of students were growing.

Nandini was so happy to see her dreams turning into reality. Within some months, the first floor of their house was ready to use. It also had a bigger kitchen to accommodate Nandini's students. They shifted upstairs with their belongings.

*****

Nandini Convinces *Maa*

It was so many months that they didn't meet Shashikala as they were busy in the construction going on. So one weekend, they both went to Nandini's place and surprised *maa* who appeared even weaker this time. There was a visible hunch in her back as she moved very slowly with each step.

Both of them disclosed their reason to come to meet *maa* this time.

"*Maa,* I will help you pack your bags. Tell me what all you need," asked Nandini.

"What are you saying, Nandini? I can't live in my daughter's *sasural*. I am still not that shameless *beta*. I am good here. There is no such issue," replied Shashikala.

"But... you can live with your son, right *maa?* There is no shame in living with your son!" said Karan.

"My son, I know you are worried about me a lot. But trust me, I am good here. And how can I leave my house, your *baba's* memories are here. It is his house which he had made with his blood and sweat," Shashikala replied sulking.

"*Maa, baba* stays with you wherever you go. He is within you. His memories won't ever leave you or me. He must be worried too in the heavens to see you all alone. He would rest in peace only when he see you happy, and you are happy with your children, right?" asked Nandini.

"And *maa,* don't worry. You will be taken care of by your daughter. All your responsibility will only be mine. Not anyone's else. You have a right on me and I have a right on you. Please, for me... for your Nandini... your only love after *baba*," requested Nandini as Shashikala appeared perplexed.

It took some time and a lot of convincing for them to make *maa* ready to live with them. Finally, she was ready to move in with them.

*****

ONE YEAR LATER...

The Arrival of Twins

After an year of building understanding and living their best couple life, Nandini and Karan welcomed their twin baby girls. They were Nandini's world and Karan's universe.

When Nandini was looking at her new born girls' faces, something rekindled in her heart – the urge to write her emotions into her diary.

She took her diary and penned down her feeling on a paper after a very long time.

Dear diary,

I had never imagined that I would go for months without writing in you. To be honest, I don't even remember where I left the last time I wrote in you.

But... today as I open your pages again, I am riding a roller-coaster of emotions. Ufff... so much had happened in this break between us. My entire life took a 360 degree turn.

Well... I do not wish to revisit the streets of my hurtful past. Whatever happened... made me a person I am today! So, let's talk about my present because all is well that ends well.

As I write this page, my newly born twin daughters are looking at me, reflecting their cute glowing happy faces.

I am grateful to God for giving me all the things that I ever wanted in life. A caring husband, a promising career and – daughters.

I still can't believe that a girl like me, who comes from a village, with a minimal education, can achieve so much in life. I have read many times that God helps those, who help themselves. Initially, I didn't believe in it because, I was doing all within my boundaries to help me but nothing worked.

But then I realised... what does helping yourself actually means. It means to break your boundaries and go beyond them, beyond your estimated abilities. And then, you will realise that you have an immense power within you. God wants you to find yourself that way and then he helps you with everything.

As a woman, I have had many realisations in this span of my married life. A woman... should always be independent, no matter what. No matter if you have a degree or not, no matter if you are allowed or not, no matter if you are supported or not... no matter if you are loved or not. There are millions of ways to make it. Just don't lose hope.

You have got your own back. It's only YOU who can change your life and the way the world perceives you.

It was only when I decided to take a big stand for myself that the world changed its perception towards me. The day I decided to take no more disrespect or harassment, I won. People changed the way they behaved with me. Everybody!

I started this journey from ashes to wings for my maa. No wonder how a mother's prayer can change a child's life miraculously. And now, with tears of joy in my eyes, I am proud to say that today, I too have become a maa for my children.

No doubt a woman is able to do wonders which men can never and one of them is to bring a life to this world, almost losing their own!

If there is only one thing that I can teach my daughters, then it would be to never tolerate oppression, disrespect, harassment, gas-lighting and belittlement from any one in the world.

To be independent and work on yourself, your goals, your desires and your dreams. BUT... always remember that... independence should never bring arrogance with it. Success should never come above family values and love for each other.

Independence only teaches a woman to stand on her feet without asking for someone's constant support. However, it should never let you take wrong decisions in life. If life gives you a second chance to correct something that is broken, always... always go for it.

Never let your independence be the reason for your regret of choosing materialism over emotions. When there is ever an option to choose between giving a second chance to your relation or letting it go because you can handle it all alone, always choose the former.

Because... some relations are for eternity!

My lovely daughter, when you both grow up... just remember your maa's words. Be bold but kind, be strong but understanding, be independent but humble... be a good life partner but never be someone's unheard housewife!

With Love,
Nandini

THE END...